THE BELLES LETTRES PAPERS

Also by Charles Simmons

Powdered Eggs
An Old-Fashioned Darling
Wrinkles

THE BELLES LETTRES PAPERS

a novel

Charles Simmons

WILLIAM MORROW AND COMPANY, INC.

New York

Portions of this book originally appeared in a slightly different form in *The Nation* and *The New Republic* under the name Frank Page.

Library of Congress Cataloging-in-Publication Data

Simmons, Charles, 1924–
The belles lettres papers.

I. Title.
PS3569.I4729B4 1987 813'.54 86-28527
ISBN 0-688-06049-8

Printed in the United States of America

First Edition

1 2 3 4 5 6 7 8 9 10

BOOK DESIGN BY RICHARD ORIOLO

To
DEIRDRE
and
MAUD

Contents

The Persons of Belles Lettres

Frank Page, *an editor and the narrator*

Aubrey Buckram, *the founder*

Winifred Garamond Buckram, *the original publisher and wife to Aubrey*

Samuel Serif, *the first editor*

Xavier Deckle, *the second editor*

Cyrus Tooling, *the original owner of Protean Publications and purchaser of Belles Lettres*

F. E. Backstrip, *the third editor*

Skippy Overleaf, *the fourth editor*

Jonathan Margin, *the fifth editor*

Ellie Bellyband, *an editor*

Ed Princeps, *an editor*

Ben Boards, *the art director*

Virginia Wrappers, *an editor*

Barry Vellum, *an editor*

Claire Tippin, *a secretary*

CYRUS TOOLING JR., *present chief of Protean Publications and son of the original owner*

MARY (TOOL) TOOLING, *his wife*

LOU BODONI, *the office manager*

CHUCKLE FAIRCOPY, *an editor*

ROSE CLOTH, *a secretary*

PHIL FLUSH, *the head of personnel for Protean Publications*

SHIRLEY BASKERVILLE, *the assistant general counsel for Protean Publications*

ART FOLIO, *a copyboy*

SYLVIA TOPSTAIN AND CYNTHIA BINDING, *his aides*

CHRISTOPHER BLANKS, *a contributor*

NEWBOLD PRESS, *the sixth editor*

THE INFORMER, *a staff member*

BOBBY QUARTO, *a copyboy*

SELMA WATERMARK, *a secretary*

THE VISITING WRITER, *a famous American author*

S. SEWNBOUND, *a Shakespeare scholar*

GARY CARTOUCHE, *a statistician of Elizabethiana*

THE BELLES LETTRES PAPERS

I

A Rich Man's Plaything

THIS INTRODUCTORY CHAPTER IS A CONDENSED VERSION of an undergraduate paper I wrote in 1982 on the history of the literary weekly Belles Lettres. It covers the years 1951–73 and the editorships of Samuel Serif (1951–54), Xavier Deckle (1954–60), F. E. Backstrip (1960–71), and Skippy Overleaf (1971–73). It does not deal with the two subsequent editors, Jonathan Margin and Newbold Press. A firsthand report on their administrations appears in, in fact constitutes, the body of this work, which is a memoir of my two years with the magazine.

Belles-Lettres (the hyphen disappeared in 1960) was founded by Aubrey Buckram in 1951, half as a wedding gift for his bride and half as a bribe. Winifred Garamond, a recent Radcliffe graduate, agreed to marry Buckram on the condition that she have her own career. She had majored in medieval history, done her honors essay on Joan of Arc, and was now contemplating graduate work at Yale. In anticipation of their marriage Buckram purchased an apartment on New York's lower Fifth Avenue (he was also looking forward to a cottage in the family compound in Oyster Bay) and didn't like the idea of his young bride commuting to New Haven. He tried to persuade her to take a degree at Columbia, but she would have none of it, saying (the remark is apparently still quoted in Cambridge): "To attend Columbia after Radcliffe would be like shopping at Macy's in a Chanel suit." So to save Winifred from "that Gothic pile surrounded by slums, like a paste pearl in a rusted setting [Buckram on Yale, quoted in a 1960 Time article about the sale of Belles-Lettres to Protean Publications], I conceived the idea for the magazine and had no trouble selling it to Winny. I didn't want to change the face of American letters, I wanted to keep my wife at home."

Belles-Lettres's offices were, literally, around the corner from their apartment, on East Eleventh Street in a brownstone Buckram bought for the purpose. Winifred's first problem was whether to run Belles-Lettres herself or take on an experienced hand. She had been editor of her high school magazine and had worked on the Harvard Crimson in her senior year; but this, after all, was a professional project. So an editor was hired, and Winifred named herself publisher (as she appears on the masthead of the maiden issue, dated September 4, 1951). Buckram was probably instrumental in the choice of editor, although he seemed to disavow this with such statements as (from the Time article): "Winny was completely and exclusively in charge. If she asked for an opinion I gave it, if not not." At any rate, the choice was Samuel Serif, twenty-seven, a classmate of Buckram's at Harvard, where Serif had been a rather flamboyant editor on the Advocate. After graduation he founded and edited Sky Writing (1948–51), a quarterly not much remembered today; but, coming as it did shortly after the war, it was watched, as all literary magazines were, for signs of an American renaissance.

Sky Writing folded in 1951 for lack of funds, and Serif accepted the editorship of Belles-Lettres. Buckram, heir to a glue and cotton fortune, is said to have put $400,000 into the magazine in the first year alone. It was to compete with such periodicals as The Saturday Review of Literature, which, although it was respected at the time, covered other cultural fields besides books; Time and Newsweek, which reviewed books but exploitatively, looking for the item that would make a good story; the little magazines, which reviewed books seriously (some said ponderously) but months, sometimes years, late; and finally the journalistically limited book supplements of such Sunday newspapers as The New York Times and The New York Herald Tribune.

"It was a wide-open field," Buckram said.

Belles-Lettres under Samuel Serif did not take the field. In the three years of his editorship its average weekly circulation was 7,000, somewhat lower in the last year than the first. Buckram himself said, "Sam Serif was and is a very bright, very hard-working chap, but he just didn't know what to do with the money I gave him. I fully understand that some of the reviews he commissioned have become anthology pieces, but people didn't want to read a quarterly magazine that came out every week. Sam and I are still great chums, and I hope he will forgive my saying that he remained an undergraduate at Belles-Lettres."

Looking at those early issues, one sees Buckram's point. Many of the reviews ran more than four thousand words; in some issues half the reviews were by current or former Harvard faculty members; and the illustrations were impertinent decorations. It seems clear that Serif, in his eagerness to put out an influential journal, suppressed his natural insouciance, the very quality that might have stood him in good stead as editor of a magazine seeking broad readership.

After three years, everyone agreed—Buckram, Winifred, Serif himself—that the magazine needed a new editor. How Xavier Deckle came into Buckram's view and how he was persuaded to take over what was essentially a rich man's plaything are important and uncertain parts of the Belles Lettres story. Buckram was quoted in Time: "Obviously there was one man in America to do the job. When you looked into it you found Deckle associated with the most important literary occurrences in America in the previous decade. He knew absolutely everyone. And he was an editor, not a writer manqué. In answer to the question of how I got him to take the job, let's just say I had ways."

Unaccountably Winifred was not interviewed for the Time article. I wrote to her in the fall of 1981, asking for her view of the Deckle hiring. Her response was generous, touching on many aspects of the Belles Lettres story. About the Deckle appointment she wrote: "Xavier was my idea, just as Sam

Serif was Aubrey's. As publisher of Belles-Lettres, with ultimate responsibility for the magazine, I received much correspondence. I have among my papers at least thirty letters from Xavier during Sam's editorship. The first merely recommended a certain reviewer. Subsequent letters—needless to say, I responded with gratitude to Xavier's interest in what was at the time an almost invisible publication—were full of comments on the magazine in particular and literature in general. All suggestions, of course, were turned over to Sam, who sometimes acted on them, sometimes not. At any rate, by the time Sam was ready to leave I was ready to hire Xavier. Aubrey did meet Xavier's rather stiff demands, but I would like it on the record, if you can arrange it, that Xavier Deckle was my choice, not Aubrey's." (Buckram failed to respond to my request for countercomment. In fairness, I must say that clarifying a point in an undergraduate paper may not have been his highest priority.)

What no one disputes is that Belles Lettres's subsequent rise to prominence and profit was due to the editorial genius of Xavier Deckle. To this day no one quite knows how he got the people he did to write for him. He said himself, "Book reviewing is a mug's game when done regularly. Sparingly it's a splendid way to lay waste an old friend or make a new enemy." One of his two greatest coups was getting Hemingway in 1959 to review, under a pen name, Faulkner's late novel "The Mansion." Considering the shape Hemingway was in and the questionable quality of the Faulkner book, the review was lucid and kind. When the reviewer's identity became known—Deckle is said to have leaked it himself—Faulkner wrote to Deckle offering to return the favor; but there were no more books from Hemingway in his lifetime. The other coup, which never saw print, was to visit Ezra Pound in St. Elizabeths in 1956 with a copy of Eliot's play "The Confidential Clerk" and to get Pound to suggest emendations. Deckle was ready to turn over an issue to the edited version, but Eliot and his publisher refused. (It is not generally known that subsequent editions of the play quietly adopted several of Pound's changes.) This was indeed Belles Lettres's golden age, and it came to a sudden, tragic end in 1960 when Deckle died in a fall from the terrace of his New York apartment. (The story given out by Buckram was that Deckle had been drinking and probably had slipped. The general feeling was that the death was a suicide. A year later evidence surfaced that Deckle that evening had picked up two sailors, who threw him from the terrace. When asked about this, Buckram said, "If it's true I can only say that Xavier died as he lived, taking chances.")

Deckle's death and another occurrence, in late 1960, led Buckram to sell Belles-Lettres to Cyrus Tooling's Protean Publications. After nine years of marriage Winifred left Buckram for a Belles-Lettres editor by the name of Pavel Faircopy. (Winifred and Faircopy quit the magazine to start a newsletter reporting on art auction prices. Faircopy's younger brother joined the staff in 1961 and was there when I came to Belles Lettres in 1983.) The double loss was too much for Buckram, and he accepted Tooling's reported $6 million. (Buckram would not confirm or deny the figure for Time, but he did say that despite all he had put into the magazine he was coming out even. Did this mean, Time asked, that he would pay no taxes on the money, to which he said, "Ask my accountant, and if he tells you I'll fire him.")

The magazine now passed into frankly commercial hands. Cyrus Tooling by an odd coincidence (although it has been suggested that the "coincidence" actually recommended Belles-Lettres to him) was publishing a line of service magazines whose names were common French words—Jardin, Théâtre, Vin. In this regard it is interesting to note that Buckram in the Time article takes credit for naming Belles-Lettres, adding, "I chose the name with a certain irony. But even so it seemed better than the other contenders, of which I recall 'Bookworm' and 'Bookbag.'"

Tooling took no chances with his choice of the next editor for the now hyphenless Belles Lettres. Into the job he shifted F. E. (Effie) Backstrip, chief of Jardin ("the magazine with ten green thumbs"). Backstrip, who was then in his early fifties, had spent virtually his entire working life with Protean and could be relied upon for a businesslike performance. Protean magazines maintained a nice balance between the needs of the reader and advertiser. Backstrip applied the formula to Belles Lettres while also trying to continue the Deckle ingenuity.

It was generally agreed, however, that the writers Backstrip introduced were, to a person, mediocre. Dwight Macdonald claimed that Backstrip's faultless taste for the second rate was a gift. Nonetheless, or therefore, circulation, which had reached 140,000 at Deckle's death, doubled in Backstrip's first three years and continued to rise at a lesser rate in the next four years. Ad revenues, too, rose in those seven years, as did the size of the issues. Even after the figures leveled off in 1968 the magazine remained healthy. At its peak Belles Lettres was getting fifty-six cents of the book industry's advertising dollar.

Backstrip was not a success with the intellectuals, to put it mildly. One of his troubles was following Deckle, who had been their darling. Near the end of Backstrip's regime a commentator said that coming after Deckle was like coming after Kennedy. From the intellectual's vantage point there seemed to be a witless naïveté or, worse, a sophisticated cynicism to all of Backstrip's editorial decisions. And the more popular and influential Belles Lettres became the more the intellectuals resented it. Articles attacking Backstrip were written by, among others, Macdonald, Paul Goodman, and Robert Lowell. Issues of two little magazines, Tiresias and Clear Water, were given over to critical analyses, parodies, and other abuses of Belles Lettres. Tiresias printed an especially damaging selection of quotations from Belles Lettres reviews, as well as an interview with Backstrip in which he described how he had become editor: "When Cyrus asked me I said, 'Hell, I had a shot at posies, I might as well take a crack at books.'" He also said, "Let me tell you right off, I'm not a literary bloke." These remarks were frequently quoted thereafter as prima facie evidence of inadequacy.

At the close of his tenure a dispassionate appraiser in the Columbia Journalism Review added an insight about Backstrip's bad press: "The people who didn't like him were used to playing what they considered hard ball. They'd beat up on someone and would expect the person to beat up on them, or try to. What drove them mad was that one of them would publish a savage attack on Backstrip and he would respond by running a glowing review of the fellow's next book. They couldn't get their teeth into Backstrip. He was either too dumb or too smart for them." What the Columbia Journalism Review didn't know was that Cyrus Tooling, who supported Backstrip through the attacks, counseled him never to defend himself (reported by Backstrip to a colleague, who passed it on to me in a letter): "When someone calls you an asshole in a magazine with 10,000 circulation only an asshole denies it in a magazine with 300,000 circulation."

Backstrip retired, or was retired, in 1971 at age sixty-two. (He died in 1976; Tooling in 1975.) A colleague said this: "The sixties were over, and Effie Backstrip hadn't done anything about them. He wasn't supposed to. But that was no excuse. Old Man Tooling wanted something or someone to say to the public, 'Look, we're young like everybody else.' Backstrip had run a very conservative show. Consequently Protean picked as his successor a very young, very bright, very unconventional sixties type. Belles Lettres was going to catch up in a hurry. It was an experiment. It didn't work."

The new editor was Skippy Overleaf, twenty-seven (the same age as Samuel Serif twenty years before); he was the current wonderchild of American journalism. Simultaneously he was senior television critic for Protean's magazine Le Tube, writing under the name Voyeur; occasional book columnist for The New Republic; stand-in theater critic for New York magazine; a favored correspondent for The New Statesman on anti-American stories; and not a month went by that two or more feature articles by him did not appear in national magazines. He had published three books and had contracts for four more. He produced so much of such high quality that Wilfrid Sheed once accused him of being identical twins. Almost everyone was delighted by the appointment. The Belles Lettres staff had not been able to effect innovations during the turbulent sixties and were dying to be let loose. The intellectuals, who under ordinary circumstances might have been wary of anyone so young and flashy, seemed pleased. Tooling obviously thought he had done something daring, even grand. "Protean Publications," he said, "is pleased and proud to turn over this august cultural responsibility to the next generation. I have been asked if I didn't think Skippy Overleaf was too young for the job, to which I say, let's remember that Napoleon commanded an army at Skippy's age." Only the book publishers were uneasy. A Doubleday executive expressed their sentiments with this encomium for the departing Backstrip: "I'll tell you exactly what Effie's strength was. He loved a good read, and when he discovered one he loved to tell people about it. And when he did he'd also tell you what the title, author, publisher, and price were and get the information right. Effie was my idea of a *bookman.*"

Overleaf proved to be, by all accounts, an erratic, part-time editor. He continued to do as much writing as before. According to one Belles Lettres editor, "Skippy gave us about a day a week—that is, if he wasn't too busy." How did the magazine get out? "By sheer momentum. Of course, Skippy's one day was full of surprises. He was a Roman candle with an extra supply of fiery balls. In his second month the Vietnam thing appeared. At the time we thought the Marines would occupy the office." The Vietnam thing was a 10,000-word review of all the contra-war material that had been published by big and small presses across the country. Its variety and extent were considerable. A good deal of it was in pamphlet and broadside form, and it included arguments that Johnson,

Nixon, and their aides should be tried as war criminals, Nuremburg-style.

Overleaf commissioned and ran this without a word of warning to Tooling, whose politics were those of most American businessmen: that is, anything that's good for, in this case, Protean Publications is good for America. He was outraged that one of his magazines had been used by an employee for ideological purposes, and he was for chucking Overleaf on the spot. He was cautioned that this would be interpreted as a political statement, and he didn't want to make political statements. The best thing he could do was wait till the matter cooled and then fire Overleaf. The Vietnam piece, however, got a very positive response; it was reprinted in almost every European country; and for a while Tooling again thought he had hired the right man.

But Overleaf and Belles Lettres were not doing their jobs. When not perverse the choice of books reviewed seemed arbitrary, and the choice of writers to review them provocative. The Village Voice, pleased that a large commercial publisher like Protean was uncomfortable with one of its editors, egged Overleaf on: "It's about time we discovered what the pot-pushers, prick-pullers, hardass women and softass men, the smack-smugglers, snow-sniffers think about books. You got it up, Skipper. Keep it up!"

What finally brought Overleaf down was the 30,000-word, step-by-step instructions by an MIT undergraduate for assembling an atom bomb. Overleaf used a whole issue to print it, with diagrams. He ran the piece under the headline "You've Written to Your Congressman, Now . . ." and in his introduction called this issue of Belles Lettres "the

Hiroshima issue." After the Vietnam affair, Tooling had given orders, not only to Overleaf, but to Protean's printers, that he was to see everything that went into the magazine. Overleaf, however, waited for a week when Tooling was away and switched the material at the last minute. The issue was sold out in half a day and fully reported in the print and electronic press. A formal protest was delivered on the floor of Congress. A New York Times editorial said that publishing the article was "an act beyond conscience or sanity." Tooling issued a public statement that "this brilliant young man has obviously been working too hard, for which I blame myself. He promises me that he will seek psychiatric help." And in fact Overleaf was reported to have gone through a difficult personal time after being relieved of the editorship.

The fifth editor of Belles Lettres was Jonathan Margin, who took over in 1973 at age thirty-nine. Like his two immediate predecessors he had been associated with Protean Publications before assuming the editorship. Unlike Backstrip he *was* a literary bloke, and unlike Overleaf he was *not* a wonderchild. The pendulum had returned to dead center. My job with Belles Lettres was the happy outcome of my college adviser sending a copy of my paper to Mr. Margin, who returned to me a very careful analysis indicating where I had hit the mark and where I had missed it, saying in sum, "But somehow you seem to have understood us. Come see me when you're next in New York." I did in the fall of 1983, and Mr. Margin was kind enough to offer me a job.

II

How Belles Lettres Worked

As soon as I joined the staff everyone wanted to know how Belles Lettres worked. Did we actually read all the books? How did we decide which ones to review? How did we pick the reviewers? These were the innocent questions. People closer to the book business wanted to know whether we told reviewers what to say and whether we changed the reviews. People in the business didn't even ask; they assumed that a conspiracy existed to control opinion, although no one was sure to what end. In thinking about these questions I'm reminded of the conversation Jonathan Margin and I had at our initial lunch.

". . . so we all have our individual tastes," he was saying.

"And thank God! What else could justify fobbing off our judgments on a helpless public? We have an odd and, I might add, attractive gathering of tempers and temperaments at Belles Lettres. Our sensibilities range from the vigorously vulgar to the exquisite and even effete. I like to think we represent a critical construct of the American readership. So that when we say yes to a book we say yes within the confines of the book's intentions. We do not say no to mysteries, we say no to bad mysteries. We do not say yes to poetry, we say yes to good poetry. And if a book maintains an opinion, nay a bias, nay a prejudice, we try to state who we are and what we stand for, and then judge the book on the quality of its argument. What I'm saying is that at Belles Lettres we are interested in the how, in the means, in the process. . . ."

Mr. Margin was a long, thin man from an old, though poor, New England family. He had a bony New England face and a deep voice enriched by self-amusement. "So you probably wonder," he went on, "how it is possible for such a group of, as I say, diverse, if not divided, personalities to put out a magazine of book reviews. I often wonder myself. For instance, what do you think happens when two members of the staff disagree about a book?"

"Don't you leave that to the reviewer?" I said.

"Ah!" He was pleased by my question. "But which reviewer do I send it to, the hard reviewer or the soft reviewer, the John Simon or the Anthony Burgess?"

"I've seen soft reviews by John Simon," I said.

"Ah! But let's say this book is not by a dead European. Rather by a living American, moreover by an American who for years has been getting away with murder. . . ."

"Heller?" I said.

Mr. Margin blanched. "I was thinking more of . . ."

"Styron?" I said.

He didn't blanch, but he did clear his throat. "Let's just say an overrated writer. In fact, you have illustrated my point. I say 'overrated writer,' but what do I mean but overrated in my opinion? So let's say there's another member of the staff who doesn't think the writer is overrated at all, and he thinks this new book is a masterpiece. Whom do we send it to, John Simon or Anthony Burgess?"

"John Simon," I said.

"All right, why?"

"He's good at masterpieces, real and fake."

"And Anthony Burgess?" Mr. Margin said.

"He's good at real masterpieces but not fake ones."

"How so?"

"He doesn't say they're fake, he just uses his fake voice."

Mr. Margin's eyes narrowed. "I can see you're a clever young man," he said.

The exchange came back to me a few months later on a Monday afternoon when the staff had gathered in Mr. Margin's office for the weekly assignment meeting. Everyone was there, with the new books he or she had read over the weekend, to make review recommendations. The exercise usually proceeded clockwise around the conference table at which we sat, starting at Mr. Margin's left with Ellie Bellyband recounting in detail the plots of four or five English novels—English fiction was her specialty—which she would eventually dismiss for review because they weren't up to the authors' previous work, on to Ed Princeps at Mr. Margin's right. Ed would cover seven or eight, sometimes ten, books of scholarly interest. His enthusiasm for all books was great, but for scholarly books very great, and it was difficult for Mr. Margin not to assign for review even the most esoteric item after Ed had claimed that it was witty, incisive, groundbreaking, written like a dream and to be ignored at our peril.

On this Monday afternoon Mr. Margin said that we would pass directly to Ed, who had something special to report on. "Ed!" Mr. Margin said with an emcee nod.

Ed always introduced what he had to say, even if it was only a word or two, with a cough, a pause, and a smile. The cough was part apologetic and part authoritative, the smile was both boyish and devilish. Today he said dramatically, "This is a *big* one." And indeed in front of him were two thick volumes of bound galley proofs.

I suppose, like me, the others thought it was a definitive study, in progress many years. Actually, it was Norman Mailer's Egyptian novel, and everyone perked up. We had been hearing about it for months, and although proofs had been circulated among the book clubs and paperback houses, the reviewers hadn't seen a thing; that is, till now.

For myself, I was a bit taken aback, since I thought it was understood that contemporary American fiction had become my "field" at Belles Lettres. However, Mr. Margin had his reasons for giving Ed first look.

"Before I begin," Ed said, "I'd like to say right off that Norman's novel is indescribable."

Ed had a disconcerting way of referring to well-known people by their first names. When it was "Pauline," "Mordecai," "Gore," you knew whom he meant, but occasionally it would be "John" or "Bill," and you had to ask John who, Bill who. Once, after being asked and telling us that the John was Updike, he explained that he had been worrying about John a lot lately and consequently felt especially close to him. (In defense of this practice of Ed's I must say that once I mentioned him to Updike and Updike said, "How *is* Ed Princeps?" and went on to tell me that Ed's full first name was Editio, which I hadn't known, adding with a sly smile, "He *is* an original, isn't he?")

Anyway, about Mailer's novel Ed continued: "It's called 'Ancient Evenings,' and I say it's indescribable because when I get done you may not have a clear idea of what it's about. So I'm going to tell you what it's *like.* It's the Old Testament written by Mel Brooks, the 'Book of the Dead' by Henry Miller, the Iliad by Woody Allen, the head of Nefertiti by Red Grooms. . . ."

"I heard it has a lot of farting and puking in it," Ben Boards said. Ben is the art director of Belles Lettres and sits in on assignment meetings to get a sense of what's coming up. "A lot of goosing too," he added.

"Speak up! Speak up!" said Virginia Wrappers, a senior member of the staff who thought of herself—and everyone else did too—as the guardian of standards. She might actually have become hard of hearing over the years, but she did have a way of making people repeat things they wanted to say only once.

"A lot of goosing too," Ben Boards said.

"What does *that* mean?" she said.

Mr. Margin injected himself, as he often did, like a carbon

rod into fissionable matter. "Ben said, Virginia, that he had heard that the new Mailer was full of vigorous vulgarity."

"I see," she said and settled back.

"I asked Ed to report on the Mailer novel," Mr. Margin said, "because he has, as we all know, a strong classics background. 'Ancient Evenings' is destined to be a controversial book, and we want to be on firm ground with it. This Mailer is not like any of the Mailers we are familiar with, not the early Mailer of 'The Naked and the Dead,' nor the middle Mailer of 'The Armies of the Night,' nor the recent Mailer of the Marilyn books and 'The Executioner's Song.' This is an entirely new Mailer, which not everyone will be prepared for. I myself feel the book is a grand experiment, of . . . how many pages, Ed?"

Ed opened the back cover of the second volume and said, "Seventeen hundred and fourteen galley pages."

"Could I see that, please," said Barry Vellum, who took care of science and poetry books for Belles Lettres, mainly because nobody else was interested. "I used to know Mailer, and I've read all his books."

Ed pushed the two volumes across the table and resumed talking. "What we have to recognize in considering this book is that Mailer has eschewed all his strengths—his deep understanding of modern society, his unmatched ear for the American idiom, his absolute mastery of narrative techniques, his quixotic readiness to fly in the face of popular prejudice, his unparalleled willingness to make a fool of himself—and it is this last attribute, if I may say, that is the most important for an artist to have . . ."

"Ed, may I interrupt?" Barry Vellum said. "I just opened the second volume to page 1231, and I'd like to read it."

"Do you think we have time for that?" Mr. Margin said.

"I think it might be instructive," Ed said.

"All right, Barry, read away!"

Barry read: "'She delighted to search out rare sanctuaries throughout Thebes. Unlike Usermare, She was not only dedicated to Amon, but to gods revered in other cities, as Ptah in Memphi, or Thoth in Khnum, not to speak of the great worship of Osiris in Abydos, but these gods also had their little temples here with their loyal priests, plus many another god my Queen would find in many another temple, and often in the meanest places—at the back of a muddy lane in a slum of Thebes with the children so dirty and ignorant they did not bow their heads at the sight of Her nor express any sign of awe, but merely goggled their eyes. [Barry made goggle eyes.] Still (the lane too narrow for Her palanquin) She plunged Her fine feet and golden sandals to the very bottom of the alley, there to have her toes washed by priests of this shabby little temple of—be it—Hathor or Bestet or Khonsu, or in finer quarters down broad avenues, past the gates of mansions with their own pillars, sentries, and privately commissioned small stone sphinx, we might pass through the slender marble columns of a "divine little temple," as She expressed it, to pay homage to Goddess Mut, who was Consort to Amon, or to . . .'

"That's page 1231," Barry said.

"Yes, indeed," Ed said, "and what do you make of it, Barry?"

"Not much."

Ed did his cough and smile and said, "I'm not surprised. Can you take a page at random from the last half of any immense work, read it out of context, and expect to come up with anything? Suppose in 1921 you read page 877 from 'Ulysses' to an assemblage like this?"

"All right," Barry said, "I'll try the first volume." He opened it near the beginning. "This is page seventy-four."

"Barry," Mr. Margin said, "you're not planning to read more, are you?"

"More! More!" Virginia Wrappers said.

"Why not?" Ed said.

"All right," Mr. Margin said. "Everyone seems interested."

And Barry read: "'In such a darkness, void of light, no move in the wind, no breath to stir a thought, the query of the Sekhem persisted. One would be judged. And time went by without measure. Was it an hour, or a week before the light of the moon rose in my mind, and the interior of my body became bathed in its light? A bird with luminous wings flew in front of that full moon, and its head was as radiant as a point of light. The bird must be the Khu. Naming it, I realized that one thought, at least, had entered my head again, and must come from the Khu—this sweet bird of the night—a creature of divine intelligence given to us in loan just so much as the Ren or the Sekhem. Yes, like the Name and the Power, the Khu was here to light up your mind all the while you lived, but in death, it must return to heaven. For, unlike the Ba and the Ka, those fourth and fifth parts of the seven souls and spirits who could most certainly perish after your death, the Khu, like the Sekhem and the Ren, was eternal. Yet, not entirely eternal, not entirely undamaged. For out of the hovering of its . . .'

"That's page seventy-four, and I don't make much of it

either." Barry pushed the two volumes back across the table toward Ed.

Mr. Margin said, "Thank you, Barry. Were the two pages in fact representative, Ed?"

"They were representative of *one* of the book's modes. There are others." But he did not elaborate, and he let the bound galleys lie in the middle of the table. I think he felt he had made an error in backing Barry's reading. He turned his attention, passively, to Mr. Margin, who said, "Well, do you have any suggestions for the reviewer, Ed?"

"I think Joyce Carol would know what to make of it," he said.

"She has a high shit threshold, but not high enough," Barry said.

"Speak up! Speak up!" Virginia said.

"Joyce Carol Oates does not have a high enough shit threshold to review Norman Mailer's new novel," Barry said loudly.

"Well, then we don't want her," Virginia said.

"Any other suggestions?" Mr. Margin said, throwing the matter open for general discussion.

It was hard to catch who said what, but some of the offerings went like this:

"How about one of those Columbia trochees, like Morris Dickstein?"

"Flaccid," someone said.

"Perhaps someone of more . . . stature," Mr. Margin said.

"Stephen Marcus?" someone said.

"Flaccid" was heard again.

* * *

"V. S. Pritchett," someone said.

"He wouldn't do it."

"Sure he would. It's Norman Mailer."

"I think we should stay in America," Mr. Margin said.

"How about another novelist, like Vonnegut?"

"What are the politics there? Have they crossed swords?"

"Vonnegut won't write for us since that review of him we ran."

"Ben DeMott would be thrilled to do it, and he's a soft touch."

"We are not interested in a 'soft touch,' we are interested in a sound judgment," Mr. Margin said and turned to me: "Frank, do you have any ideas?"

"Would we be interested in John Simon?" I said.

"I won't abet savagery," Mr. Margin said.

"Then I think I have someone," I said. "A writer of accomplishment and international reputation, who is creatively venturesome himself, without jealousy and considered by many to be a genius. . . ."

"Goethe's dead," Ed Princeps said.

"But Anthony Burgess isn't," I said.

There was silence around the room. I watched Mr. Margin's face to see if he recalled our early interview. I don't think he did, because finally he said, "That's a *good* idea, Frank, a *damned* good idea. Do we all agree?"

We did.

"Then it's Burgess . . . for a *major review!* Claire," Mr.

Margin said to Claire Tippin, his secretary, who had been taking notes through the meeting, "get a wire off to Tony soonest."

After the meeting I got Claire alone and asked her why Mr. Margin was being so nice to Mailer.

"I think" she said, "because Mailer agreed to review that new biography of himself. It would be a newsy piece, you have to admit."

"And in return . . ." I said.

"Nothing in writing," she said, "but understood."

And that's more or less how Belle Lettres worked. Also, I must report that at the next meeting Barry showed up with his Bodley Head edition of "Ulysses" and read us page 877, which was from Molly Bloom's soliloquy and contrary to Ed's assertion might have done all right in 1921:

"come 3 or 4 times with that tremendous big red brute of a thing he has I thought the vein or whatever the dickens they call it was going to burst though his nose is not so big after I took off all my things with the blinds down after my hours dressing and perfuming and combing it like iron or some kind of a thick crowbar standing all the time he must have eaten oysters I think a few dozen he was in great singing voice no I never in all my life felt anyone had one the size of that to make you feel full . . ."

Three or four times Virginia Wrappers asked Barry to speak up.

III

Who the Fuck Is Harold Brodkey?

Mr. Margin called me into his office and asked me to sit down. He called staff members into his office in order not to be overheard. When he asked them to sit down, though, someone was in trouble. This time it was Mr. Margin.

"I don't know if you're aware of this, Frank, but Tool dislikes me."

"No, I wasn't," I said, which was not entirely true. I had been hearing that Mr. Margin was on the way out, or at least down, to be shifted to a subordinate position on Mer et Terre, Protean's travel magazine.

"Yes, she dislikes me *intensely*."

Tool was Mary Tooling, wife of Cyrus Tooling Jr., present publisher of Protean and son of the founder. Mrs. Tooling had a special interest in the company's cultural magazines. I enjoyed watching her at the monthly meetings she held with the Belles Lettres staff. She was a demonstrative woman of about forty-five, suspicious, well dressed, with black eyes that met yours only to indicate displeasure. She did most of the talking. Occasionally she asked a question but rarely listened to the answer. Or she listened for a certain answer and nodded if you hit on it. Or she listened not to what you said but to what she thought you meant. For instance, someone would complain that he needed more work space, and finally she would say, "All right, you can have the raise."

"I don't know why she dislikes me so," Mr. Margin said. "I follow her directions to the extent that she can explain them to me. I don't argue with her. I don't bad-mouth her. It's true that we come from different backgrounds. But, after all, this is Protean Publications, where the most diverse strains in American journalism have gathered in harmony and profitability." This last word didn't sound right, and Mr. Margin paused to let it settle into his diction. "Frank, in the short time you've been at Belles Lettres you've proved to be very observant. Do you know anything that might . . . ameliorate the situation?"

He was asking for gossip. I said, "What do you actually think of Mrs. Tooling?"

He sat upright. "What do I think of Mrs. Tooling? I think she is a . . ." It was an awfully long search for the right word, which turned out to be "ruffian."

"Could it be that Mrs. Tooling dislikes you because you dislike her?"

That hadn't occurred to Mr. Margin, and he looked startled at the thought. When he recovered he said, "Do you think there's anything . . . to be done about it?"

"If you tried to be nice to her now she'd know you were faking. It would only be a sign of weakness. I'd just play it by ear, Mr. Margin."

"By ear," he said. "Yes, and let's keep our eyes peeled and our antennae up at the meeting today, shall we? Needless to say, Frank, I'd like you to keep this thing completely . . ."

"Completely," I said.

What a rotten position to be in at Mr. Margin's age, I thought. He is a perfectly well-respected editor. He has been a member of the Grolier Society for ten years and is now on the admissions committee. He rolls with the punches from publishers like Lyle Stuart, whose books Belles Lettres doesn't review, and he listens sympathetically to people like Don Fine ("Jonathan, you know I never complain, but . . ."). Also he is able to get all but the best writers to work for him, and at fees considerably lower than the general magazines pay. Still, no one is eager to give a merely adequate forty-nine-year-old editor a job at the salary Mr. Margin has worked himself up to. It seemed to me that he would have been better off had he gone into teaching. By now he would have been head of a department at a good college or president of a mediocre one. In either case he would have been dealing with people he understood rather than with Mary Tooling.

* * *

Mrs. Tooling was waiting for us in Protean's corporate conference room. She sat at the head of the long table, and Mr. Margin took his place at the foot. They looked like man and wife, with the rest of us like children along the sides.

"Marge," Mrs. Tooling began, "I had lunch yesterday with Dick Snyder. Dick Snyder," she said to the rest of us, "is the head of Simon and Schuster. Dick said that Belles Lettres stinks. I said, 'Dick, what do you mean?' 'Stinks,' he said. 'S-t-i-n-k-s.' This is the head of Simon and Schuster talking, Marge." Mrs. Tooling leaned over the table for Mr. Margin's reply, and the staff turned as if watching a tennis match.

"You don't understand, Tool," Mr. Margin said. "When a book publisher criticizes us in that manner what he is doing is softening us up so that the next time around we owe him something. That's all this is."

We turned back to Mrs. Tooling. Mr. Margin's first words—*you don't understand*—had been unfortunate. Mrs. Tooling said, "Let me tell you something, Marge. When congressmen, senators, Supreme Court justices, the President of the United States want to know certain things they call me or my husband. *I understand.*"

"I understand too," Mr. Margin said after a pause.

Mrs. Tooling continued, "So Dick Snyder, head of Simon and Schuster, says Belles Lettres stinks. What could I say? That it doesn't stink? Could I honestly look Dick Snyder in the eye and say to him in all honesty, 'Dick, Belles Lettres does not stink'?"

She was asking a real question, and she pointed to me.

"Sure," I said.

"Oh, I could have *said* it. Nobody's going to put me in jail for perjury. But let me ask you directly, Does Belles Lettres stink or does it not stink?" She pointed to Barry Vellum.

"I wouldn't say it *stinks,* Tool," Barry said.

"I wouldn't either," Mrs. Tooling said. "I would say that it has no smell at all. When a critic on Théâtre goes to a show and has a good time he says, 'I went to this show, and I had a good time. If you go to the show you'll have a good time too.' What's the matter with book critics? They *hint.* If a book is good I want to *hear* it." Mrs. Tooling raised her voice. "Sing it out: 'I like this book. This is a good book.'"

"Enthusiasm is cheap," Mr. Margin said, "and not always convincing."

"Who's talking enthusiasm?" Mrs. Tooling said. "I'm talking communication."

Poor Mr. Margin! Here he thought he had sold out, and Mrs. Tooling was telling him he hadn't sold out enough.

She went on: "Belles Lettres is the most powerful literary magazine in the world, and *you don't use the power.* I don't want you to inform taste, serve taste, improve taste. I want you to *make* taste. I don't want Belles Lettres to guess who's going to win the Nobel Prize, I want Belles Lettres to *award* the Nobel Prize."

"Actually we do have an impact on the Pulitzer," Mr. Margin said. "This year I'm one of the judges. . . ."

"I'm not talking behind-the-scenes. I want it out front. I want Belles Lettres to say who shall live and who shall die. And no maybes."

I thought this was too much, so I said, "Mrs. Tooling, I have an idea."

"Call me Tool! Let's *hear* it!" She had worked herself up.

"Why doesn't Belles Lettres establish who the twenty-five best writers in America are? One, two, three, four . . ."

Mrs. Tooling stared at me and said, *"The twenty-five best writers in America. One, two, three, four."*

"And no ties," I said.

"And no ties," she said. "What's your name?"

"Frank Page, ma'am, but I was only kidding."

She didn't hear me. "Marge, this is what we need. We'll make the front page of The Times. There'll be editorials, counterlists. *What's* your name?"

"Frank Page."

"Margin!" Mrs. Tooling shouted.

"Yes?"

"Do it!"

Mr. Margin nodded.

Mrs. Tooling rose. "Now we're getting somewhere. One, two, three, four. . . ."

"And no ties," I said.

"And no ties!" she said.

It was one thing for Mary Tooling to mistake my irony for an editorial suggestion, but on the way back to the Belles Lettres office members of the staff came up to compliment me. Ed Princeps said the idea was a "corker." Ben Boards, the art director, said we'd have to sit down and work up some glitzy graphics. Virginia Wrappers said that the feature "would put a lot of people in their places." Only Mr. Margin looked sour, and when we got back he didn't have to say, and I didn't have to be told, that he wanted me in his office and he wanted me to sit down.

"How could you do this, Frank?"

"I was being ironic," I said.

"You can't be ironic with a . . . ruffian."

"I know that now, Mr. Margin. But maybe the idea really could get attention for Belles Lettres. Couldn't we think of it as a *jeu*?"

"Frank, you have not understood the purpose of Belles Lettres or indeed of any advertiser-supported magazine. It's true that we point out the difference in excellence among books. It's true that at the end of a decade we hope to have drawn attention to the one or two genuine talents that have emerged. But week to week we try to point out as few differences as possible."

"I don't follow you, Mr. Margin."

"Every week is another ball game. Every week we try to turn up three or four books that readers will want to go out and buy—or at least feel that they should go out and buy. We don't say to the reader, 'This is a pretty good book being published this week, but why not wait till next week, when there will be a really good book?' Do you understand?"

"Yes, sir."

"So, if we tell our readers that the twenty-five best writers in America are so-and-so and so-and-so, how can we tell them in a week when none of these writers is bringing out a book that they should buy a book by the twenty-sixth best writer in America, or, more to the point, by the one hundred and twenty-sixth best writer in America? It's all well and good to play the Faulkner-Hemingway-Fitzgerald primacy games—dead writers don't write books—but, if I may use Mrs. Tooling's diction, we're talking cash, and flesh."

"I'm genuinely sorry, Mr. Margin. But couldn't you explain all this to Mrs. Tooling? She wants Belles Lettres to make out as much as you do."

"Under other circumstances I might be able to. In fact, under other circumstances I wouldn't have to—whoever was in charge would have understood what I've just been saying. But, if I were to go to Tool now, she would get the message well enough—but she would also see that from my own staff had come an idea that was finally going to do me in."

"Isn't that a little . . . extreme?" I said.

"No. There is something else about magazines you don't understand. You're a young editor. You see a magazine in terms of its editorial content. But a magazine is a vehicle that advertisers rent. Our editorial content could be changed in a month if the advertisers and readers wanted it. Along with the content, of course, would go the editors. Not that they couldn't make the changes. But their sacrifice would be a gesture to the industry. . . ."

Just then Claire Tippin, Mr. Margin's secretary, announced that Mrs. Tooling was on the phone. As if carrying a weight, Mr. Margin went to his desk. I rose to leave. He motioned me to sit.

"Yes. . . . Right. . . . Yes. . . . Okay. . . . However, if we publicize this before it's ready the job will be more difficult. Every publicity girl in the industry will be over here on behalf of her authors. I suggest we wait until it's done, then publicize the hell out of it. . . . Yes. . . . His name is *Frank Page*. . . . He's already an assistant editor. . . . Double? . . . All right. . . . Yes. . . . Yes," Mr. Margin said, and put the phone down with a little bang.

He turned to me. "You are to 'implement' the idea. Also, your salary is doubled. That puts you within striking distance of mine."

I nodded. What could I say?

"Also, as I pointed out to Mrs. Tooling, if word gets out that we're doing this, every publicity girl, and boy, will be over here offering lunches, dinners, weekends in the country, their very persons, to see that their authors prevail."

"That doesn't sound as bad as it sounds," I said.

"Well, yes, you're young," Mr. Margin said.

The next morning, first thing, Mr. Margin assembled the staff in his office. "Despite our ambivalence," he said, referring to the fact that the venture was not his idea or to his liking, "I see no reason that it should not be prosecuted with taste and wit. It is a commonplace that a magazine cannot be edited by committee, but I do want this to be a group effort. The list we arrive at should be both defensible and ingenious, responsible yet not obvious, contain surprises and conviction, imply an aesthetic and still welcome the exception, be American without being parochial, reflect traditions as well as experiment. . . ."

Mr. Margin was too good at this sort of thing. There were times when he got caught up in his own rhetoric. However, he finally came to the point:

". . . So I want each of you to make up your own list of the twenty-five best writers in America today. And, please, submit your choices alphabetically. We'll have to worry all too soon about the one, two, three, four of it. At present I merely want to see the shape of your thinking. One thing:

Because we should do this with a minimum of external influence I suggest we keep it inside the office." There was a stirring, and Mr. Margin looked carefully around the table. "Do I gather that some of you have already been busy on the phone?"

There were no demurrers.

"So be it," he said with a sigh. "Frank here," he nodded to me, "has been detached from his regular duties to bring this matter to a speedy and satisfactory conclusion. Please get your lists to him as soon as possible."

Sure enough, the next day Page Six of The Post announced that Belles Lettres would soon choose the twenty-five best writers in America, adding—maliciously, I think—that nominations could be made by phone or in person to Jonathan Margin, editor.

The day after, Edwin McDowell wrote a story in The New York Times saying that, contrary to rumors in the publishing industry, Belles Lettres magazine did not—repeat, not—plan to pick the twenty-five best writers in America. However, the next day he wrote another story to the effect that Belles Lettres was indeed publishing such a list, the confusion having arisen from the vehemence with which the editor, Jonathan Margin, in a phone interview had denied soliciting nominations from readers.

New York magazine's Intelligencer column ran an item saying that Belles Letters, "the influential literary weekly, definitely *is,* as denied and then confirmed by The Times, naming the twenty-five top American scribes. The brass at Protean Publications, owners of Belles Lettres, are counting on the idea to liven up what they feel to be the lackluster performance by editor Jonathan Margin. The choice of the twenty-five immortals will be made by the entire staff under the direction of Belles Lettres's new assistant editor, Frank Page, whom the biggies at Protean like the looks of."

Alexander Cockburn, in his Nation column, said: "Jonathan Marginal, editor of Belles Lettres, the literary snews magazine, hopes to wake us all with his version of the twenty-five best writers in America. No need, Marginal. We can name them in our sleep. Start with Bellow, end with Updike, and one gets you ten Charles Bukowsky doesn't make it. Snews on, O faithful readers of Beautiful Letters!"

Within a few days I had all the lists and brought them to Mr. Margin.

"How are they?" he said.

"Interesting."

"That sounds ominous."

"Not really. Take a look!"

He did and for rhetorical purposes read aloud the list of Lou Bodoni, the office manager:

"'John Ashbery, Ingrid Bengis, Paul Bowles, Rita Mae Brown, Susan Brownmiller, Guy Davenport, Marilyn French, Marilyn Hacker, Jill Johnston, June Jordan, Paule Marshall, James Merrill, Kate Millett, Robin Morgan, Marge Piercy, David Plante, Adrienne Rich, Paul Robinson, May Sarton, Alix Shulman, Kate Simon, Valerie Solanis, Gloria Steinem, Alice Walker, Edmund White.'"

Mr. Margin looked up in wonder.

"It's a document, I agree," I said.

"Yes," he said and seemed to sink into thought for a few seconds. "Well," he then said, "you know, of course, that Lou Bodoni is a radical feminist."

"I didn't know that. She seems so pleasant."

"The thing about radical feminists," Mr. Margin said, "is that they start in fear, convert it to hatred, which they finally turn into contempt. When all the fear has been transformed into contempt they can be quite pleasant, like Lou. Watch her sometime when there is an argument between two of the men editors. A little involuntary smile plays around the mouth. I see Stalin smiling like that when Roosevelt and Churchill had words. But if you wonder why I'm interested, my second wife was a radical feminist."

"Is she no longer a radical feminist or no longer your wife?"

"Oh, no longer my wife," he said. "I'd like to keep in touch with her, but she's still working on some of the hatred. . . . Do you realize that Virginia Wrapper's list doesn't share one name with Lou's?"

"I noticed that," I said.

Again for rhetorical reasons he read Virginia's list aloud: "'Nelson Algren, Louis Auchincloss, James Baldwin, Hortense Calisher, John Cheever, Edward Dahlberg [Mr. Margin paused, then went on], Joan Didion, J. P. Donleavy, William Gaddis, William Gass, Paul Goodman, Elizabeth Hardwick, Lillian Hellman, James Jones, Jack Kerouac, Harper Lee [he paused again], Alison Lurie, William Maxwell, Walker Percy, Reynolds Price, J. D. Salinger, Diana Trilling, Lionel Trilling, Robert Penn Warren, and Thornton Wilder.'

"Frank, didn't you tell Virginia that this was a list of living writers?"

"I thought that was understood."

"Ah, well," Mr. Margin said. "On the other hand, Chuckle Faircopy's list is almost dead center. Bellow to Updike, as that chap in the Nation said, the one with the nasty name."

"Chuckle's list really surprised me," I said. "I thought it would be the most eccentric of the bunch. By the way, what does he *do* over there in the corner besides write headlines for the reviews?"

"That's all he does," Mr. Margin said and leaned back. "Chuckle predates me, but I understand that at one time he contributed a great deal to Belles Lettres. Headlines were only part of his duties. But, what with time and age, he fixed on the headlines. Every now and then he shows me his work sheets—twenty pages for one headline. He tells me that sometimes after working all day and at home through the evening the final version comes to him in a dream. He'll wake and write it down and then won't be able to get back to sleep from the excitement of it."

"Are the headlines that good?" I said.

"They seem quite ordinary to me," Mr. Margin said. "He recently showed me one he had worked on for two days. It was a review of a history of New York City. It was 'New York Was Like That.'"

"What do you make of his immodest proposal?" I said. "Is it based on his headline writing?" Between Ralph Ellison and Allen Ginsberg, Chuckle had named himself as one of the twenty-five best writers in America.

"Some years ago," Mr. Margin said, "he published a few novels. They came and went. When I was appointed editor here he gave me signed copies. I put off reading them, but I could see that he wanted comment, so finally I told him that they were beautiful and profound."

"Did that satisfy him?" I asked.

"I think so, although he added, 'and funny.'"

"But you never read them."

"No. But, for God's sake, don't tell him!"

"Of course not," I said. Nor would I have. Chuckle, whose brother, Pavel, had run away with Winifred Buckram more than two decades before, was obviously a sad case. He looked to be in his late fifties, a tall, thin, balding man with half-glasses and a weathered face. I knew he wrote the headlines for Belles Lettres, but I had no idea that he spent the whole week on them. The way he arched over his typewriter, suddenly pouncing into composition, I was sure he was up to more than headlines.

"Well, what do we do, Frank?"

"We have to make up this list ourselves. Let's take Chuckle's names, smooth out the bumps, add three or four eye-catchers, tell the promotion department to warm up the suspense, and publish the damn thing under a short, humble, pompous introduction."

Mr. Margin nodded and sighed philosophically.

The temptations from publishers who wanted to influence the list (Mr. Margin had expected them to be irresistible) were not forthcoming. A cutie-pie publicity girl asked me to lunch, saying that she wanted to discuss one of her authors. I pointed out to her, as she must have known, that Belles Lettres editors could not accept lunches from publishing people. She asked if that included lunches made from leftovers and served by amateur cooks in their abodes. I said I didn't think so, and we made a date. More for his amusement than anything else, I mentioned the lunch to Mr. Margin.

"Who is the author?" he said.

I told him.

"He'll be on the list."

"I more or less told her that," I said, "but she wants to talk."

"I suspect she wants to add *you* to *her* list," he said, and on the morning of the day of the lunch, he told me I had been working too hard and should take the afternoon off. It turned out that not only did she really want to talk about her author but she was marrying him the following week.

I prepared a list from Chuckle Faircopy's, adding about ten names so that Mr. Margin and I had room to move around in, and considering the difference in our ages, we had an easy time of it. We struggled some over John Barth, Donald Barthelme, and Thomas Pynchon. Without telling who was for whom, I can say that we traded off gracefully.

I showed the list to Chuckle, to tell him that the choices were basically his and to warn him that his name would not be on it. He said that since he doubted that either Mr. Margin or I had read his books he was not offended.

Mr. Margin called the staff into his office. His secretary, Claire Tippin, had made copies of the list and distributed them like menus.

"First of all," Margin said, "I want to thank you for your extremely conscientious choices. Your lists constitute some of the most interesting reading I've done in recent weeks. Each was a brain scan. I seemed to see not only leanings and backgrounds but hard strivings to understand this often confusing American scene. The list you have in your hands is a weighted consensus. The 'weight' comes from Frank and me and represents perhaps two or three names that did not appear on any of your own lists. I'm sorry the list is not longer, that it does not include each and every writer that each and every one of you put forth. Such a list would be an invaluable document, far more interesting than this 'essence' that we shall show to the public. Such a list would have revealed the true taste of the editors of the most influential literary publication in the language. And consider: Suppose, just suppose, we had such a choice from a similar group of London intellectuals in 1616, the year of Shakespeare's death. What a contribution that would have been to the history of ideas!"

Mr. Margin went on like this for a while and finally asked for comments.

"Why is Mary McCarthy, who has lived in France half the time, on a list of the best writers in America?"

"By 'in America,'" Mr. Margin said, "we merely mean 'American citizen.' Just as I. B. Singer is on the list although he came here as a young adult and doesn't write in English."

"In that case, George Steiner is an American citizen living in England. Why isn't he on the list?"

Mr. Margin nodded for me to answer.

"Many reasons," I said.

"If by 'best' we mean 'most important,' surely Michael Harrington should be on the list."

"'Best' only means 'best,' I'm genuinely sorry to say," Mr. Margin said.

"I feel that we have pointedly excluded engaged writers. Surely Norman Podhoretz is as influential as any writer in America."

"Then we'd have to include Irving Kristol and Hilton Kramer," I said. "You wouldn't want that."

"There are no critics on the list. I want to nominate Alfred Kazin again."

"Again?" Mr. Margin said.

"Are we avoiding experimental writers?"

"As I understand it," Mr. Margin said, "an experimental writer is a writer whose experiment has failed."

"Where is Renata Adler?" someone asked.

No one seemed to know.

Mr. Margin and I gave the list to Mary Tooling. She called us to her office the next day. "Do you want to know what my husband said?"

We nodded.

"My husband said—and pardon my French—my husband said, 'Who the fuck is Harold Brodkey? And where the fuck is Herman Wouk?'"

"About Brodkey," Mr. Margin said, "we thought that a few offbeat names might add a certain . . . spin to the list."

"And Herman Wouk?" Mrs. Tooling said.

"There are many writers in America," Mr. Margin said.

"Okay, but for myself," Mrs. Tooling said, "where the fuck is . . ." and she mentioned five writers *she* thought should be on the list.

"If you wish," Mr. Margin said.

"I wish," Mrs. Tooling said. "And don't put them at the top. Slip them in. And another thing: This is alphabetical. We were talking one, two, three, four."

"Tool," Mr. Margin said, "that's impossible. Who is better, Bellow or Updike? Mailer or Roth? It's impossible to decide."

"Decide!" she said and rose in dismissal.

What we did was to take the last twelve names on the adjusted alphabetical list and alternate them with the first thirteen. Then we took the last eleven on the intermixed list and placed them above the first fourteen. A cryptographer would have discerned what we had done, but no one else.

Of course, the rest is history. The list, as Mrs. Tooling had prophesied, was commented upon around the world. I reprint it here for meditative purposes:

"Allen Ginsberg, John Updike, John Hawkes, Kurt Vonnegut, Edward Hoagland, Eudora Welty, John Irving, Richard Wilbur, Mary McCarthy, Herman Wouk, Norman Mailer, Woody Allen, Bernard Malamud, Donald Barthelme, James A. Michener, Jacques Barzun, Arthur Miller, Saul Bellow, Lewis Mumford, Thomas Berger, Philip Roth, Peter De Vries, I. B. Singer, E. L. Doctorow, and Anne Tyler."

The Times of London said: "A startling affirmation of America's riches! Here is a roster that shouts 'Vigor!' England, thy child hath surpassed thee."

L'Express: "The twenty-five names hold few surprises to devotees of American literature. But the order! The ranking contains such play of point and counterpoint, such wit, so sardonic and yet so correct! That Ginsberg, the holy man of the 1960s, should emerge as the premier American writer! And that he should precede the great Updike! What outrage! What wisdom!"

Literaturnaya Gazeta: "Twenty-five writers of assent. Where are those who have asked the questions? Where are Robert Coover, Gore Vidal, Seymour Krim?"

After it was done and a great success, I again congratulated Chuckle Faircopy on his original list.

"You want to know something," he said, "I got it from the biographical entries in this," and he picked up a copy of the American Heritage Dictionary. "There are about thirty-five living American writers here, and I picked twenty-five."

"Twenty-four," I said.

He smiled serenely and said, "There'll be other editions."

IV

Mr. Margin and Women 1

I WAS HAVING LUNCH WITH MR. MARGIN. WHEN THE drinks came he said, "Frank, have you ever been in love?"

"Sure," I said.

"It's an awesome experience."

"It sure is."

"Awesome," he said, and I realized I was to understand that my being in love was not to be compared with his being in love.

So I said, "Sort of awesome."

"It has happened to me four times," he said.

"Four!"

"The first and third time I married the woman."

"And the second?"

"The second, I often think I should have."

"Why didn't you?"

"It has occurred to me, strange as this may sound, that she was too nice."

"Too *nice!*" I said, feigning surprise. Or let me put it this way, I was surprised that he had that much insight into himself. A friend and contemporary of his had told me that his first wife had been very rough on him, also that she was a little cracked. She put dead birds under his pillow. "I asked him," the friend said, "what he did when that happened, and he said that he'd say to her, 'Louise, what is this?' and she would say, 'Don't you know what that is, Jonathan?' and he would say, 'It's a dead bird,' and she'd say, 'If you know it's a dead bird why do you ask?' and he'd say, 'What I mean is why did you put it under my pillow?' and she'd say, 'If you don't know that, I can't help you.'" The second wife was the radical feminist, and once when he was drunk Mr. Margin told me that she held her legs together when they made love. I asked him how that was possible, and he said, "Just."

"But you mentioned four times," I said.

"I'm in love again now," he said with what seemed like a combination of pride and uncertainty.

"That's terrific," I said.

"I'm in love with," and he paused in an uncharacteristically stagy way, "Claire."

Claire Tippin, Mr. Margin's secretary, was a perfectly good secretary, cheerful, efficient, proper as a butler, with, as Barry Vellum put it, Mount Rushmore tits.

"I suppose you're wondering how it all happened."

"Indeed I am."

"It's quite a story," he said, smiling into his drink and swirling its contents around until some spilled. "It all began right there in the office one Monday evening. Everyone had left but Claire and me. . . ."

Actually it was an ordinary story. It seems that after the first fateful Monday they stayed in the office every evening for the rest of the week. They couldn't go to her place because a friend was visiting, and they couldn't go to his because the radical feminist former wife kept a key and had a way of showing up. So they did whatever they did in the office. Needless to say, Mr. Margin did not go into details, but I had heard the details from members of the staff in talking about their own experiences. "You know the old Morris chair in the storeroom. . . ."

After their week in the office they went away for Saturday and Sunday, then spent the nights of the next week at her apartment, from which she had flushed the guest.

Then she went off for ten days in Hawaii.

"It had been arranged for a long time," Mr. Margin said. "She couldn't get out of it. At first, after she left, I thought we had simply played out a strong, sudden mutual attraction, and to tell the truth I was looking forward to being alone to recollect it in tranquillity, so to speak, but after one day I was beside myself. I had fallen in love, for the fourth time in my life. The amazing thing is that exactly the same thing happened to Claire on her first day in Hawaii. She realized she had fallen in love. For me, I know I desperately wanted to declare myself. I didn't know where she was in

Hawaii. I got her mother's number from personnel, but she didn't even know Claire had gone to Hawaii."

"Did Claire call you?" I said.

"No, but the very instant she got back I fell upon her."

"And she liked being fallen upon," I said.

"Yes, and that's how it happened."

"I think it's terrific," I said. "To be in love . . ."

". . . and to be loved in return."

"What more could one ask?"

"Nothing," Mr. Margin said.

But there was something.

"There is something," he said.

"That I can do?"

"She went to Hawaii with a friend, which she candidly and voluntarily admitted. The trip had been planned for months, the tickets bought, the hotel reservations made. . . ."

"You said."

"So there was nothing else but to go."

"Was it with a man?"

"I honestly don't know," Mr. Margin said.

"She won't tell you?"

"It's not that she won't tell me. It's that she doesn't want to discuss it. She says it doesn't concern the 'usness of us,' which in one way is perfectly reasonable. . . . Frank, I am subject to obsessive thoughts."

"I can see that."

"You said it yourself—why didn't she call me when she discovered she loved me?"

I was about to say that maybe she was too busy. What I did say was, "But why worry now? The arrangements were made for ages, the past is the past, the main thing is the present and the future."

"Those are almost her very words."

"And they're correct," I said.

"I know they are, but . . ."

"You want me to find out."

"Frank, this is very embarrassing. If I didn't know how . . . human you were. . . ."

"How can I do it?"

"Ah!" he said. He had a plan. "Ask her to lunch."

I nodded.

"Say you're going to Hawaii."

I nodded again.

"You want her advice. Which hotels, which islands. I know her. All you have to do is set the proposition and listen. Everything will come out. . . ." He paused from shame, not that he was asking for help, but that he was asking me to trick her. Nonetheless, he said, "Will you help me?"

"Of course I will," I said. "I'll do whatever I can. But I must do it my own way."

"I understand," he said.

"It's not that I don't want to do it your way, it's that I'd be no good at it. But let me try something. Trust me!"

"I trust you," he said, nodding his head to convince himself that I would not destroy his love affair and him along with it.

"And now I think we should talk about something else," I said and held up my glass to toast the proposal.

"To something else!" he said.

* * *

You don't go up to a secretary and ask her to lunch as you would a fellow editor, at least not a secretary who looks like Claire Tippin. If you did and she agreed, when the time came, as you walked from the office together, stood waiting for the elevator together, returned an hour late to the office together, buzzed from the what-the-hell brandy with coffee, everyone would cock an eye and vice versa. So if you had something in mind you wouldn't ask her to lunch, you'd wait around one evening when she had extra work to do, wander over, and say, "I could use a drink, how about you?" In fact, that was probably how it started with Claire and Mr. Margin, except I suspect it was Claire who did the waiting around and wandering over.

At any rate, I solved the problem by asking her to lunch while Barry Vellum and Mr. Margin himself were standing at her desk, and the fact that I didn't get a look from Barry meant that the invitation was taken innocently, except perhaps by Claire, who I think wondered why I was inviting her to lunch in front of all these people.

As we talked in the restaurant I tried to keep her from coming to mistaken conclusions. I mentioned girlfriends so that she wouldn't think I was making a pass; when she brought the office up I changed the subject so that she wouldn't think I was looking for gossip; in response to her question whether I thought everyone on the staff was "in the right job, slot-wise," I said I did, so she wouldn't think I was feeling her out for another position (I sensed some disappointment when that possibility disappeared). Why I didn't let her come to a false conclusion I'm not sure. Perhaps I felt duplicitous enough taking on Mr. Margin's mission in the first place.

However, I did commit two dishonesties. The first was the lively interest I expressed in her trip. I smiled and smiled and listened to more than I wanted to know about the flora, fauna, sky, beaches, weather, and people of Hawaii. My second dishonesty was the remark, "But weren't you lonely?" to which she said no, she had gone with a friend, who then became part of the story. "My friend" and "my friend's" appeared two, three, four times in single sentences instead of the he, she, him, her, his, hers that English craves. It was a virtuoso performance in gender avoidance, from which I concluded that her friend had been male and very heterosexual. Then at coffee she astonished me by saying, with her eyes lowered, "You're close to Mr. Margin, aren't you?" I said I guess I was. And she said, "I am too," and touched the back of my hand with her fingertips. She had figured out what I was up to, wanted to reassure me, and me to reassure Mr. Margin.

I may have given the impression that Claire was a big woman. But, apart from the Mount Rushmore effect, she was fragile, small-boned, with delicate wrists and Botticelli hands. In fact, her face had that serene and open Botticelli look, which to me represents a very appealing combination of beauty and stupidity. After she had touched the back of my hand I wondered whether, if I brought my hand to her cheek and neck, she would bend her head toward it like a cat. Then the image occurred to me of her opening her mouth to bite my hand and instead licking it, and I decided that she was worth Mr. Margin's discomfort and that I would do whatever I could to help him keep her.

Mr. Margin and I had arranged to have lunch the day after I met with Claire, but he couldn't wait and took me out for a drink that evening. I told him more or less what she had said, not how strenuously she had tried to conceal her friend's gender, but simply that I hadn't been able to discover it. I saved her tender remark for the end, and when I repeated it he looked a little like a Botticelli himself. He even touched the back of my hand in gratitude.

On Monday morning two weeks later Mr. Margin sat me down in his office and said, "You know my policy, that anyone on the staff is welcome to write for the magazine so long as the assignment is appropriate."

I nodded. Something was up.

"We definitely want everyone to feel that he or she is part of the team."

I nodded again.

"And if, now and then, by writing an article, reviewing a book, assuming that the individual is capable of doing a creditable job, there is no reason why he or she should not, so to speak, 'get into the act.' Oh, I understand that there are editors who say, 'We are the editors, they are the writers.' But I don't agree with that. I feel that when an editor writes he or she learns about writing and therefore learns about editing. . . ."

For myself, I had learned about speeding Mr. Margin up. A little bum-shifting or ankle-scratching was usually enough.

This time something turned up in my eye. I pulled my eyelid out and down and rolled my eyeballs.

"Are you all right?" Mr. Margin said, leaning forward. "Would you like a handkerchief?" He took one from his breast pocket by two fingers and held it out.

"It's fine," I said, accepting it and continuing to roll my eyeballs. "It's out," I said and swabbed the corner of my eye. "Wow!" I added.

Mr. Margin gave me time to reassemble my attention and then said, "To get to the point, Claire has asked me for the new Graham Greene."

I nodded.

"Not for a copy of the *book,*" he said, "she wants to *review* it."

"Review it!" I said.

"Review it," he said.

"Is Claire really up to the assignment?"

"Why don't you see for yourself," he said and took from his desk a typescript of five or so pages.

"You mean, she's *done* it?"

"Yes," he said, "after a fashion."

Claire was an impeccable typist, but these pages were full of handwritten insertions, deletions, and substitutions, with many crossing lines of redirection. The pages looked like sections of a road map. The emendations, of course, were Mr. Margin's attempt to bring the piece around.

"Would you look it over?" he said, as casually as he could

"Of course."

"And would you," he added, "peer through my scribblings to the . . ."

". . . heart of the matter?" I offered.

"Le cliché juste," he said with the saddest smile.

Claire was clearly an ambitious young woman. Earlier, it came back to me, she had gone for recognition to Lou Bodoni, Belles Lettres's butch office manager. Lou responded enthusiastically, and for quite a time the two of them were passing papers back and forth like money changers. I later learned that the papers had been Claire's literary efforts criticized by Lou, redone by Claire, recriticized by Lou, and so on. Lou actually said to me one day, "You know, Claire really has something up here," pointing to her head. And that's not the only place, I thought but did not say because I knew Lou enjoyed bringing out the worst in men. At any rate, Lou had not been in a position to help Claire with much more than advice, whereas Mr. Margin could actually launch her. Or maybe he could, which was what we were about to consider.

Her review was worse than I had expected. I hadn't read the new Graham Greene. Apparently she had snatched the galleys as soon as they arrived in the office, taken them home, and written her review over the weekend. Nor had I read anything substantive about the book. So I was as ignorant as any subscriber to Belles Lettres would be, and after going over Claire's piece I still didn't have a clue as to the book's content.

You see many kinds of bad writing in this business. There is the kind with plain mistakes: *infer* for *imply, fulsome* for *abundant, disinterested* for *uninterested, aggravate* for *irritate.* An editor is used to it, and although he wonders why the writers of this writing persist he understands how they prevail—the editor infers that the abundant errors are the result of uninterested teachers, isn't too irritated, and corrects them.

Then there are the rush-on writers, who sweep away distinctions of usage. They are difficult bad writers because after the tautologies have been excised, the Rube Goldberg sentences dismantled, the non sequiturs reasoned with, there isn't much left, and the editor who first read the piece, probably in the spirit of its composition, is left wondering at his former enthusiasm. Had it been the martini at lunch, the lateness of the day, the forgiveness that comes with lengthy service?

Then there is ambitious bad writing, which prefers *empathy* to *sympathy, myself* to *me;* takes a chance with *religiose* for *religious, elemental* for *elementary, nubile* for *zaftig* (Barry Vellum defended *nubile* as meaning a woman with big nubes); avoids the ultimate preposition at all costs; connects separate sentences with a colon (as if to celebrate the logical connection of the second to the first); and finds a place for *indeed* in every paragraph. Most of these inelegancies result, strangely, from a striving for elegance and, when corrected, help satisfy, more than almost any other activity, the editor's need for self-esteem. One such striving brought forth the word *impedimentae,* for which the staff invented the rhetorical term "the double plural" and which Mr. Margin was persuaded to leave in the review as a curiosity.

But to correct errors the editor must know what the writer had in mind. Usually this is easy because most bad writing tends toward talk of one kind or another, and the intention of talk is clearer than any prose but the best writing. With Claire's review, however, you didn't know what she meant. Things would go along for two or three sentences, then she would say, "The characters in this book exist for the sake of their prejudicial influence on reality"; or, "Good and evil function here to the detriment of most, if not all, subjective implications"; or, "In Mr. Greene's world we must think of salvation as subsumed damnation."

I started by retyping a clean (if I can put it that way) copy of Claire's review so that I could look at it without the presence of Mr. Margin's panicky editing. I went at it three evenings in a row, Tuesday sober, Wednesday tipsy, Thursday drunk, but couldn't get a purchase on it. Wednesday Mr. Margin greeted me with hopeful urgency. Thursday he obviously had passed a sleepless night. Friday I allowed him to invite me into his office.

Claire's desk was just outside, so he closed the door. "Is it as bad as I thought?" he said.

I nodded.

"Worse?"

"It's nonsense," I said.

"Is there anything we can do?"

"Can't we simply tell her it's unpublishable?"

Mr. Margin's silence was painful, so I said, "Okay, I'll take care of it."

"You can?"

"I can."

"Are you sure?"

"I'm sure."

"I won't ask you how."

"It's part of my job, Mr. Margin."

"We know better than that," he said.

I got a copy of the Greene novel. It was called "The Pathetic Fallacy" and concerned a liberal Israeli newspaperman who takes up the cause of the Palestinians by reporting on the wretched quality of their lives on the West Bank. The stories are published in an extreme leftist Israeli paper and are picked up and printed throughout the Arab world. The new Labor Party prime minister was a boyhood friend of the journalist, who is being mentioned for the Nobel Peace Prize, and must decide whether to follow the advice of certain cabinet members and have the journalist dispatched or chance a split in his party. The problem is solved when the CIA agrees to do the job because the journalist's influence is stirring up the moderate Arabs against Israel.

I wrote a review on Saturday, rewrote it on Sunday, and handed it, under Claire's by-line, to Mr. Margin first thing Monday morning.

"This is excellent," Mr. Margin said, "but it bears no resemblance to what Claire wrote."

"Just say you touched it up," I said.

"Claire is no fool."

"Trust me, Mr. Margin. Actually this is what she wanted to say."

"But it's so clearly in your words and manner."

"That's just it. I'm sure she wanted to write in my style."

"You're outrageous."

"Necessity is the mother of outrage."

Mr. Margin paused, thinking, but he was sitting up straight for the first time since the problem began.

"I'll do it," he said.

"It'll work," I said.

"Of course it will," he said and sighed the sigh of the saved.

I saw Claire reading the review as I went off to lunch at midday, and from the rhythm of her typing when I returned I knew she was pleased. That evening I caught sight of them outside the building, meeting for what I assumed would be a relaxed supper.

When the review ran, Greene's American editor called to ask who Claire Tippin was and then invited her to lunch, where he showed her a letter from Greene saying that the Belles Lettres review was the only intelligent one the book had had but pointing out that the novel was not a retelling of the Christ story since the Christ story is a positive or negative metaphor for the life of everyman. "Avoid the obvious if you wish to be saved," he ended with. Claire borrowed the letter and showed it around the office. Greene's publisher reprinted the entire review in The New York Times "as a public service," and Claire was suddenly a minor New York figure.

Nothing I had written had ever received so much attention, and Mr. Margin was embarrassed that I was not getting the credit. "I can't even give you a raise," he said. "Your last one put you well ahead of everyone else in the office. But tell me what I can do."

"Let me take you to lunch," I said.

* * *

"I had hoped we could simply eat and chat," Mr. Margin said, "but I'm afraid this thing with Claire isn't over." He handed me a memo from Mrs. Tooling:

"Two questions: Since when do we commission secretaries to write book reviews? And since when do we keep people capable of writing such reviews secretaries for five years?"

I wrote on the bottom of the memo: "I am frankly surprised that I must remind you, of all people, of Belles Lettres's long tradition of hiring talented people for clerical jobs so that they can learn about us and we can learn about them. Claire Tippin has been on the staff for five years, not as a secretary only but as secretary to the editor, thus in a unique position to observe the workings of the magazine. When we hired her she was (age), practically a girl. Now she is (age), a young woman mature and experienced enough to take on fuller responsibilities. I have had my eye on Claire for a long time. When the chance arose I urged her to grasp it. She has vindicated not only my faith in her but her faith in herself. She has also vindicated Belles Lettres's tradition referred to above."

Mr. Margin read what I had written and said, "I could sign this without changing a word. But there is another complication. Claire automatically opens my interoffice correspondence and has read this. Suppose you were Claire and had read this, what would you do?"

"If I were Claire and had read that, if I were Claire and had read that . . . I'd ask for the next Updike."

Mr. Margin was astounded. "This *morning* she wanted to know when the new Updike was being published."

"We could help her again," I said.

"No, this charade must stop."

"What's the answer then?"

"For the moment, another bottle of wine."

The answer came from Time magazine in the form of an offer to Claire to be a staff writer. Mr. Margin advised her to accept, explaining that the taint of the secretary would always attach to her at Belles Lettres, and she did.

"But how will she handle it?" I said to Mr. Margin.

"They'll find out she can't write and make her an editor. Actually that's how I became an editor."

"And, if I may ask, how do you feel about all this?"

"About her leaving? The French call making love the little death. A Frenchman well into middle age, I'd say, invented the phrase, which alludes not to the swooning effect of the experience but to the realization that it will not go on forever."

It was an answer of sorts.

On her last day we threw an office party for Claire. It was almost totally an affair of goodwill. Belles Lettres had not sent anyone off to glory in some time. There were only two sour notes. Lou Bodoni had composed a fable called "A Sale of Two Titties," which she read aloud. And another memo came from Mrs. Tooling, which Mr. Margin took me aside to show to me. It asked why Mr. Margin, after "discovering" Claire Tippin, was letting her go to a competitor, especially in light of the fact that Protean Publications was currently defending a class-action suit brought by its women employees for discriminatory hiring and pay practices.

"Tell her you felt she wouldn't want to meet Time's $63,000."

"Is that what Claire's getting?" he said.

"Who knows? But it will quiet Mrs. Tooling."

A month or so later I asked Mr. Margin if he was keeping in touch with Claire.

"I'm afraid not," he said. "The choice was not entirely mine."

"I'm sorry," I said.

"Yes," he said, "and I seem to be suffering a strange mixture of . . ."

". . . memory and desire?"

"Le cliché juste," he said.

V

Mr. Margin and Women 2

CLAIRE TIPPIN'S REPLACEMENT WAS AN EXCESSIVELY PLAIN young woman by the name of Rose Cloth.

Mr. Margin interviewed twenty applicants, mostly women but some men. Near the end, Phil Flush, head of personnel, lost patience. "You won't tell me what you want, Margin. You turn them down and you won't tell me why. I'm sending you one more, and that's it." He sent Rose Cloth, and Mr. Margin hired her.

"Flush must have thought I was looking for a bimbo," Mr. Margin said to me. "Actually I was bending over backwards. If there was anything attractive—physically, that is—I said no instantly."

"Were all the others attractive?"

"Heavens, no! Did you see the big one? She lit up a cigar in my office."

"None of the young men looked like they smoked cigars," I said.

"One of them was quite beautiful," Mr. Margin said.

"The blond with small ears."

"You noticed the ears. He would have brought out every latency in the office. No, Miss Cloth will do very well."

She didn't do well at all. Her steno and typing were not up to Claire's, but the real problem surfaced one day when she and I were leaving the building together and I asked her how things were going. She was looking thoughtful, which was why I inquired.

"Mr. Page, may I ask you a personal question?"

"Sure."

"What kind of person is Mr. Margin?"

"What kind of personal question is that? But what kind of person in what kind of way?"

"In a personal way."

"He's a person, like everyone else. Maybe if you tell me what's on your mind I can answer you better."

"I think he's getting personal with me."

"You mean you think he's making a pass?"

"Yes."

I took a deep breath. This could be trouble. Everyone knew about Mr. Margin and Claire. "Can you tell me what Mr. Margin did to make you think this?"

"A woman can feel it."

"I understand that, but more specifically."

"The way he looks at me, the things he says to me, his tone of voice, his whole attitude."

"That's a lot."

"Yes, it is, it certainly is."

"Well, I'll tell you, Miss Cloth, I know Mr. Margin pretty well, and he's just not that kind of person."

"Maybe not to you," she said and walked off.

I phoned Mr. Margin at his apartment that evening and asked if I could come over. We lived on the same street, with Central Park between. I had a rent-controlled place on the West Side, he had an expensive co-op on the East Side. Occasionally I had dinner with him there, cooked and served by a Colombian couple who didn't speak English.

Tonight he took me into the living room, where coffee and a tray of liqueurs were waiting. He was so gracious I kept putting off the Rose Cloth business. But women were in the air.

"My first wife gave me this place, you know."

"I didn't know that," I said. This must have been the dead-bird wife.

"Yes, after she left, her lawyer sent me the papers, out of the blue."

"Generous."

"Considering she was a cruel woman. Of course, she could afford it."

"Rich."

"Very. I was a young man when I met her and thought it the highest good fortune to have fallen in love with a rich woman. So did my mother. She often said to my sister, 'Would you rather be a poor man's slave or a rich man's darling?' and there I was, mutatis mutandis, answering her question. Nothing I had ever done pleased her so much as my falling in love with Louise—not the lead in the undergraduate production of 'L'École des maris,' not even my summa. My father took a different view. He said he hoped I would not have to get a second job. I asked him what he meant. 'You'll be working for Louise full time,' he said."

"Was that the case?"

"No, but her cruelty kept me on my toes."

"What kind of cruelty, if you don't mind my asking?"

"No, no, I don't mind. It was a long time ago. Well, I discovered this aspect of her character once early in the marriage when we were about to make love. She said she had been reading about women in a Chinese village overrun by Japanese soldiers during World War II. It's a familiar story. The women put razor blades . . . inside themselves. Some of the women were beaten to death when the soldiers discovered what they had done. As I say, we were about to make love, and I was only half listening until she said, 'You wouldn't kill me if I did that, would you, Jonathan?'"

"What did you say?"

"I didn't say anything. I did, however, find it difficult to make love. In fact, thereafter I had to . . ."

"Feel your way?"

"Exactly."

"How long were you married?"

"Eight years."

I winced.

"Yes, I know. At dinner parties she sometimes set a separate table for me, telling the guests I was too young to eat with them."

"Did you actually sit at the table?"

"Yes. I tried to make a joke of it. The guests who were used to us went along with the joke."

"It seems bizarre."

"It was, but, you see, I was in love with Louise. Wait, let me show you something." He got up and left the room. Either his foot had gone to sleep or he had had a few before I arrived.

The room looked like old New York money—eighteenth-century European furniture acquired in the nineteenth; a large Persian and, besides the floral and sporting prints, a Hudson Valley landscape, a Mary Cassatt, a Prendergast beach scene, and two muddy oils, lit from above, of forebears.

Mr. Margin returned, as I thought he would, with a color photograph of Louise, a startlingly handsome woman, with high cheekbones, big even teeth, and sculptured lips, which, if the color was true, were purple; she was smiling down at a black and white cat she held.

"You see what I mean," Mr. Margin said.

Did I see why he loved her, or did I see that she was cruel?

"Sweet cat," I said.

"Her first words in the morning in bed were always to complain about something I had or hadn't done, often in my sleep; her second words were endearments to the cat. I came to resent the cat terribly. There's not much you can do when you're in love."

I took advantage of his meditative pause to introduce the Rose Cloth business.

He was astounded. "Frank, I give you my word as a gentleman . . ."

"Of course," I said. "The thing now is to decide what to do."

We considered ignoring it. If the woman was deranged it would soon show. But suppose word got to Tool. She would certainly use it against him.

"Perhaps I should take her to lunch, and we could simply talk it over," Mr. Margin said. "Often an open, forthright engagement of the problem . . ." and so on. I pointed out that probably she'd refuse the offer and then could claim that he had made definite advances. In the end we decided that we should both stay alert and that he should treat her with the utmost formality, looking at her only when he addressed her, ignoring her presence if she happened to stay after hours, leaving the premises immediately if he found himself alone with her. Also, I would pass along to her any complaints he might have about her work.

We went on drinking till quite late, discussing many subjects, none of which that night was his second wife.

Speaking, or not speaking, of radical feminists, when I arrived in the office the next morning Rose Cloth was deep in conversation with Lou Bodoni, who, I was learning, took every opportunity to be of service to female colleagues. When Mr. Margin arrived I told him about it, suggesting that we immediately get Phil Flush over and have it out with Miss Cloth.

Mr. Margin used the executive house phone: ". . . the new girl you sent me. . . . New *woman*. . . . I know all about the class-action suit, Phil. We can talk about it another time. Right now I want to talk about Miss Cloth. . . . Yes, I know you sent me twenty. I'm not blaming you, Phil. . . . Phil. . . . Will you listen? I think we have a sex harassment suit forming here. . . . Of course not. . . . Nothing. . . . Absolutely nothing. . . . Look, just get over here!" Mr. Margin put the phone down hard, missing the cradle.

Phil Flush, erect, with his belly out, always looked to me like the spokesman for an alien invading force, especially in someone else's office.

Mr. Margin called Rose Cloth in, closed the door, and the four of us sat down at the conference table. She was a stiff little creature. She made me think of a vengeful mouse.

"It has always been borne in upon me," Mr. Margin began, addressing us all like an after-dinner speaker, "that, try as we might, we remain essentially strangers to one another. Even after years of intimacy, years of reciprocal scrutiny, a single word, a single gesture, a single facial expression will reveal to us a facet of another human being that we never suspected and change our entire concept of him or her, so that if we can err after years of observation consider the possibilities of misjudgment after only six days of intermittent proximity, and that during busy working hours, when we are all absorbed, each in his or her duties . . ."

I snapped my clipboard.

"What I'm getting at, Miss Cloth, is that Mr. Page has told me that you are disturbed at what you sense to be a certain lack of propriety in my dealing with you. Is that correct?"

"That is correct."

"Yes, well, when I learned this my initial impulse was to go to you immediately and assure you, give you my word as a gentleman, that not for the slightest instant was there even a hint of impropriety in my thoughts. Then it occurred to me that thoughts after all are secret, and it might be more to the point to invite you here, along with Mr. Page and Mr. Flush, so that you could tell us in your own words just what it was in my speech, actions, or manner that provoked these feelings."

She answered like a coached witness. "Yes. When Mr. Flush interviewed me he as much as told me what to expect."

"What to expect!" Flush said.

"Please don't deny it. You said, and I'm quoting you word for word, you said, 'Mr. Margin is a *difficult* man, but he'll be all right *once you get to know him.*' There could hardly be a clearer signal."

"How am I difficult, Flush? I don't see that."

"Well, Marge, maybe *difficult* is not the word. . . ."

"The point is," I said, "that, whatever the right word, you were definitely not pimping for Mr. Margin."

"I should hope not," Flush said.

"I should hope not as well," Mr. Margin said.

"What else aroused your suspicions, Miss Cloth?" I said. "There must have been something else."

"When *you* interviewed me," she said, pointing a tiny white finger at Mr. Margin, "you told me what was expected of me *in the office.* Then you stood up, and your dress was not affixed."

"My *what?*" Mr. Margin said.

"Your dress was not affixed."

"Do you mean Mr. Margin's fly was open?" I said.

"I do."

"Is that all, Miss Cloth?"

"I then learned about my predecessor."

"What did you learn about her?"

"What he did to her."

"What did he do to her?"

"He seduced her and then kicked her out."

"Miss *Cloth!*" Mr. Margin said.

"Is that what Miss Bodoni told you?" I said.

"And others."

"Miss Cloth, I can assure you . . ."

I held up my hand, and Mr. Margin stopped. "Thank you, Miss Cloth. I think we can take it from there." I went to the door, held the knob, and she left.

"Bodoni must go," Mr. Margin said after the three of us had looked at one another for a while.

"Can't do it," Flush said. "She's leading the class-action suit."

"Then get her out of my department."

"Can't do it. Harassment."

"Suppose I throw her out bodily?" Mr. Margin said.

"Harassment, definitely."

"Let's see Rose Cloth's résumé," Mr. Margin said disgustedly. Flush unclipped it from his board and handed it over.

"Flush, it says here she has a degree from William and Harry. Did you *read* this? Did you *check* it? That woman is not right in the head."

The meeting ended in a gabble of overtalk. After Flush left, Mr. Margin said, "No more of this now, Frank. Come to my place tonight for dinner."

As I left Mr. Margin's office I saw that neither Rose Cloth nor Lou Bodoni was at her desk, and I assumed they were again conferring.

That evening Mr. Margin told me that Shirley Baskerville, Protean's assistant general counsel, would join us after dinner. Since there would be plenty of business talk then, we pointedly discussed something else, Mr. Margin's second wife, Bala.

"Her father," Mr. Margin explained, "was a history buff, and Bala was born on the hundredth anniversary of the battle of Balaklava. I don't think her name actually affected her character, but it perhaps indicated her father's character. Like boys named Lance and Damien—the names don't affect them, but the mothers who gave them the names do. At any rate, Bala was a nest of ideas, some of them quite extreme."

"We're not talking about not wearing bras, are we?" I said.

"No, no. To give you a notion, she said she had trained herself to urinate standing up."

"Is that possible?"

"I never actually saw her do it. She claimed to have taken a course with a woman in the Chelsea Hotel. It had to do with muscle control. She asked me, by the way, if, as a mark of solidarity, I would urinate sitting down."

"Did you?"

"When it was convenient. I didn't really mind that sort of thing. Some of Bala's ideas I found amusing, and others I actually endorsed. I'm a feminist, you know—or was until that Bodoni person entered my life. What I found difficult to deal with was Bala's behavior in public places, like elevators. She would not allow a man to step aside for her to get off first, and sometimes she would run into a man as ideational as herself. Stop by stop they would go up and down the elevator shaft, neither willing to exit before the other. One day I was riding along with Bala and such a chap, and he asked me if I belonged to this. . . . He used the common obscenity for a female. I replied that we were together, yes, but that I took strong exception to his language, and either he would apologize or I would punch him out. Well, Bala hit me, saying that she did not expect such sexism from any husband of hers. She was complicated."

Shirley Baskerville was a small woman in her mid-thirties; she had a long pointed nose that seemed to draw her eyes together. When Mr. Margin introduced me they closed horizontally as well, to a suspicious squint.

"And you've been with Protean how long, Mr. Page?"

"About a year."

"Only a year," she said.

"It seems like five," I said.

"Only five," she said.

"Frank is my right hand," Mr. Margin said reassuringly.

"You realize, Mr. Margin, this is a very delicate matter."

"I thought it was indelicate," I said.

"I think we can trust Frank, Miss Baskerville. But I don't

see it as delicate or indelicate. The woman is disturbed. Flush observed her. He must have told you."

"Flush was not at all clear," she said.

"Not clear! How do you mean?"

"What I mean is that what is also not clear is your record."

"I didn't know I had a record, Miss Baskerville. Where is this record recorded?"

"I won't bandy words with you, Mr. Margin. I will tell you that we cannot afford a scandal of the sort that this Cloth affair promises. We are defending a class-action suit brought by a number of women employed at Protean. The danger is not in the potential judgment but in the publicity. Sixty-one percent of Protean's readers are women. If we are found at fault we jeopardize that readership. I want you to hear a sentence from Miss Cloth's complaint."

"What complaint?"

In answer Miss Baskerville drew a paper from her briefcase and read: "I fail to understand how American women can patronize a product prepared by their victimizers. The only explanation is that they are unaware of the facts. I intend to make known to each and every female subscriber to Protean Publications just whom they are giving their money to." Miss Baskerville looked up at us, I thought, accusingly.

Mr. Margin was trying to maintain his composure. "Would you care to read the whole statement?"

"If you wish. 'Dear Mr. Tooling . . .'"

"Mr. *Tooling!*" Mr. Margin said.

"Yes. 'Dear Mr. Tooling: You should be aware that a highly placed and powerful executive of Protean Publications has been guilty of acts of flagrant sexual harassment. Beginning with my initial interview, through my first week as secretary to Jonathan Margin, editor of Belles Lettres, I have been constantly subjected to innuendo, ogling, lip-smacking, hand gestures, and one instance in which Mr. Margin's trousers were left suggestively unadjusted, all of which have caused me deep mental anguish. It is well known that Margin has a history of such behavior. How could you continue to keep an individual of such depraved character in a position from which he can prey upon innocent women?' and here follows the sentences I quoted. The complaint goes on: 'In consequence, I am preparing a detailed schedule of offenses, and lest you should consider this a product of my imagination you should know that there is a corroborative witness to Margin's outrages, herself a longtime and trusted Protean employee. Thanking you for any consideration you can give this matter, I remain . . .'"

"Miss Baskerville," Mr. Margin said, "surely you understand that Miss Cloth did not compose that document herself."

"That's not the point, Mr. Margin."

"It's pure lawyer language."

"*That's* the point, Mr. Margin."

Checking into Rose Cloth's background, personnel discovered that, like the college degree, much of the rest of her résumé was invented. In fact, the period in which she claimed to have been a secretary at Psychology Today was actually spent in a state mental hospital. Nonetheless, the affair did not do Mr. Margin any good.

VI

Belscam

WHAT I THINK BROUGHT MR. MARGIN DOWN WAS THE affair that became known around the office as Belscam. The copyboy was discovered to have been selling review copies to a dealer in used books on rather a grand scale for rather a long time. The copyboy, Art Folio, was forty-six years old and had held the job for twenty-nine years. His salary was $348 a week; his take-home from the review copies was about thirty grand a year.

Folio had come to Belles Lettres when he was seventeen, during Xavier Deckle's regime. Before his arrival it had been the practice at the magazine to take the copyboy fresh from a good college—the son of a friend of an editor, say—give him a look at editorial work, and after a few months send him on his way with a reference. At some point it was suggested that what Belles Lettres needed was a person to run copy to the printer pronto, unwrap incoming books from publishers, gofer coffee in the morning and beer in the afternoon, and take calls when the editors were busy. (In fact, soon after Folio was hired he made a certain name for himself by answering the phone with, "For whom does the bell toll?")

When Folio started at the magazine his experience had been six months as office boy for The Messenger of the Sacred Heart, a Catholic subscription monthly. When some people began to think that Folio was too old for the job he was stoutly defended by Phil Flush, an ethnicity expert, who liked to explain that he always favored Catholics for jobs subject to pilferage, bribery, and embezzlement. "Especially jobs with no future," he said. "Many's the better-qualified Jewish person I've turned down for such a job. I will say, though, that when a Catholic goes wrong he goes very wrong. I'm referring, of course, to certain Italian-American types, or, to be more specific in a general way, to certain Sicilian-American types. But, all told, I'll stand behind a Roman Catholic for a job with high temptation and low potential."

Mr. Margin was put on to the scam by purest chance. It seems that Folio got his review copies out of the office not by carrying them, which would have taken a wheelbarrow, but by mailing them to three false addresses. The addresses had changed over the years, but the final ones were: "Mr. Christopher Blanks," at a local post office box; "Mr. C. P. Broadsides," in care of Folio's girlfriend, Sylvia Topstain; and "Mr. Eric Blair," a name listed on Folio's home mailbox.

Christopher Blanks was a real person who conducted a monthly column on self-help books for Belles Lettres, Folio's thinking being, presumably, that if the mail clerk actually read the magazine, the familiarity of the name would allay suspicion. In the same way, C. P. Broadsides was an occasional reviewer of sexology books. As for Eric Blair, Folio later told me that he picked that name because it sounded literary.

One might guess that it was the Eric Blair that caught Folio up. Actually it was Christopher Blanks. Blanks for years had been coming into the office once a month to pick up his self-help books, which Folio put aside for him among the hundred-or-so review copies that arrived at Belles Lettres's office each day. This last time, however, Blanks decided to mail the books to himself rather than carry them home and therefore took them to the mailroom, where the Puerto Rican mail clerk pointed out to Blanks that the books were being sent to the wrong address.

At first Blanks thought the mail clerk was being rude, especially since he spoke in Hispanic singsong—"Meester Blanks, I theenk you have a wrong address here, a wrong address, I theenk you have it here." But there happened to be in the mailroom a Blanks package, which the mail clerk brought forth to prove his point. Blanks wanted to open it immediately, but the mail clerk insisted on the presence of a higher authority and called Mr. Margin to come attest that Blanks was who he said he was.

The package was found to contain, at list price, four hundred dollars' worth of fancy titles—unreviewable reference, art, and technical volumes—none of them suitable to

Blanks's column. Mr. Margin, Blanks, and the mail clerk retired to Mr. Margin's office, and Shirley Baskerville was summoned.

Once Mr. Margin explained Belles Lettres's mailing operation, which was entirely Folio's responsibility, everything seemed pretty clear. But Miss Baskerville warned: "Knowledge of guilt is one thing, proof is another." She then said that the contents of the Folio-to-Blanks package would be recorded and all the books marked after the manner of ransom money ("a small X on each page one hundred"), the bundle resealed, and sent to its destination. She also said that she would have a man at the other end to see who picked it up and, if possible, photograph him ("Excuse me, photograph the *person,*" she said desexingly). She also said that all mail emanating from Belles Lettres's office would be examined and, if necessary, opened, the contents recorded, etc. She pointed out that while the case was under investigation Mr. Margin should in no way modify his usual treatment of, or dealing with, Folio "or anyone else in the office," she added, giving Folio the slight benefit of the doubt. "And I hardly need say that this matter must remain absolutely confidential. On the one hand, we don't want the guilty party to fly the coop. On the other hand, we don't want Belles Lettres to be sued for libel."

Two weeks later, Mr. Margin, Miss Baskerville, and I gathered in Mr. Margin's office, and Folio was summoned. "Sit, Art, please," Mr. Margin said benignly. "Do sit down. This may take a while. I believe you know Miss Baskerville, assistant general counsel."

"Not personally," Folio said, eschewing a place at the conference table and arranging himself instead in the depths of a collapsed easy chair. He crossed his legs, put an elbow on the arm of the chair, the ball of a thumb under his chin, and the end of the attending index finger to the tip of his nose. I couldn't help but notice that the rest of us had to turn our chairs to face him. Had he been reading Michael Korda, or did this come to him naturally? The latter, I decided later.

He was a small, wiry man with black curly hair and blue eyes, always an interesting combination. If I didn't know what he had been up to he might have struck me as a feisty loser, with a touch of self-protective irony around the mouth. But, as it was, he made quite a different impression, and I realized I had never really noticed him at the front desk. He wore a checked jacket, tattersall shirt open at the neck, flannel trousers, and soft-leather loafers, which on a mere clerk would have been too sporty, but on an entrepreneur made you think of the flats on a weekday afternoon, and the clubhouse at that.

"It has come to our attention," Miss Baskerville began, using notes, "that a number of books, sent by publishers to the offices of Belles Lettres for review purposes, have been directed by an unauthorized person or persons into the hands of a book dealer or dealers specializing in resale to the public at reduced cost. It has also come to our attention that these books (which on receipt at the offices of Belles Lettres become the property of said magazine) were mailed, at the expense of Belles Lettres, to three fabricated addresses. In the last two weeks a total of nine packages were sent from the Belles Lettres offices to one or another of these addresses. The nine packages were opened, their contents witnessed and recorded, and then sent on to their postal destinations. I have here in my hand a list of said contents—103 books, with a retail value of $2,306.95. Two of the three packages sent to 'Christopher Blanks' arrived at the intended post-office box and were duly picked up. Although our operative was unable to photograph the person who claimed the packages, the operative surreptitiously visited this office and identified the claimant as Arthur Folio. I have in my hand an affidavit to that effect. Two of the three packages sent to 'C. P. Broadsides' in care of 'Sylvia Topstain' presumably arrived at their destinations. I say 'presumably' because their contents were subsequently traced to a further point, which I will come to in a moment. Finally all three packages sent to 'Eric Blair' were delivered to the residence of Arthur Folio, as witnessed and sworn to by the doorman at the residence of said Arthur Folio.

"The complete contents of these seven packages, plus thirty-seven other books believed to have been mailed earlier to one or another of the above-mentioned addresses, were delivered by Sylvia Topstain to the MyShelf Bookstore of this city on Tuesday of this week. Miss Topstain was paid in cash the amount of $600.49 by the manager of said store, who has made an oral statement to the effect that Miss Topstain and, before her, one Cynthia Binding sold to the MyShelf Bookstore on a biweekly basis for eleven years—that is, the life of the bookstore to date—so-called 'review copies' of recently published books, whose retail value amounted to an approximated $20,000 when the sales began eleven years ago and to an approximated $120,000 in the past year. We have evidence that both Miss Binding and Miss Topstain have been intimately associated with Arthur Folio, Miss Binding for at least four years, which association came to an end seven years ago, and Miss Topstain for the seven subsequent years, continuing into the present. We have, in fact, an oral statement from Miss Binding attesting to her dealings with the MyShelf Bookstore and her relationship with Arthur Folio as well as an expression of willingess to make a sworn statement to that effect. Have you anything to say, Mr. Folio?"

"You mean about Cynthia Binding?" Folio said.

"No, I mean about this entire affair," Miss Baskerville said.

"Aren't you going to read me Miranda?"

"I am not the police, Mr. Folio, although I venture the opinion that you will have your chance to talk with them. For the present I would like to know whether you have anything to say about these allegations at this point in time."

"Sure. First of all, I'd like you all to know that I think you did a great job on this, especially you," Folio said, pointing to Miss Baskerville. "Also, I'd like you to know that there used to be some nice people here. Not private detectives. If they thought you were fooling around a little, they'd call you in and ask, if you know what I mean."

"And you told them?" Miss Baskerville said.

"I was never called in. But sure. If, like, they thought someone was pushing a few books, they'd say, 'Hey, cut it out,' and that would be that."

"We're talking about more than a few books, Mr. Folio," Miss Baskerville said.

"How about you call me Art, and I call you Shirl?"

"Suit yourself, Mr. Folio. I'm more interested in what you have to say about the allegations."

"The allegations. Okay. The allegations. Well, I started this job at $42 a week—$42 a week, if you know what I mean. Which was $3 more than I was making before. But I'll tell you something. The guy who was editor then, Mr. Deckle, was all right. I mean, he *cared.* He used to say to me, 'Arthur, I enjoy your hair. It's one of the things I look forward to on my way to the office.' He kept telling me I should change my name to Mario. 'All the waiters at the Century Club are named Arthur. You should be Mario.' I told him Mario Folio sounded a little fruitio, which broke him up. He was all right. But the allegations. Okay. So publishers were falling all over themselves to send Mr. Deckle personal copies of their expensive books, and he always had them sent home. I wondered what he did with all the books. You know what he did? He sold them. A bookstore sent a truck around every month to pick them up. But there were still a lot of books coming in that no one wanted. Textbooks. Foreign books. And I started taking them home, one, two at a time. One night Mr. Deckle and I were going down in the elevator, and he asked me what I was reading there. It was a book on schizophrenia—thirty-two bucks. I told him my sister had schizophrenia, was why I was interested. He said that was a great tragedy, and he wanted to know whether she was an attractive person like myself. I don't have a sister, but I told him she had the face of an angel and the body of a chorus girl. He said he could well believe it and gave me a little pat on the can. I mean he *cared.*"

"That's very interesting, Mr. Folio, but perhaps you could

tell us more about how your book-selling operation developed," Miss Baskerville said.

"Don't you wonder why I'm handing this to you on a platter?"

"I assume you're making a clean breast of it."

"You're cute, Shirl," Folio said, and gave her a big smile. "So there's no more to tell. You got it all down with sworn statements and fingerprints. You don't need anything from me."

"There must have been a transition from taking a book or two to the operation we have here today."

"Sure, it took time. It grew, like any business."

"Then essentially you admit the allegations."

Folio held up a hand. "You're pushing me, Shirl. I didn't sign anything."

"No, but there are three of us present, who heard you confess, and our sworn statements to that effect would be tantamount in a court of law to a signed admission of guilt."

"So what are you going to do, Shirl?"

"Do you see any reason why we should not turn the matter over to the authorities?"

"Yes," Folio said, "I see a reason."

Mr. Margin, who had slumped down in his chair during the exchange, now spread his hand over his nose and mouth like a mask. He knew something was coming, as I did, if not exactly what.

"I got another operation here," Folio said.

Mr. Margin and Miss Baskerville looked at each other, then back at Folio. Folio waited, seeming to want a formal question. So I asked it: "What *is* the other operation?"

He smiled at me. He knew it wasn't my affair, and it was as if he too were an observer and only Mr. Margin and Miss Baskerville were principals.

"It's been a smooth operation," Folio said.

"Why not tell us about it," I said.

"All right, I will. I sell places on the best-seller list."

"Sell places on the best-seller list!" Mr. Margin and Miss Baskerville said in concert.

"Five grand a spot," he said, and again waited.

"Go on!" Miss Baskerville said.

"Since you ask. First of all, I compile the reports from the bookstores, right? All the shit work, right? There are fifteen spots on the fiction list and fifteen spots on the nonfiction list, right?"

We nodded. Mr. Margin had sunk even lower in his chair, and his hand was now covering one eye.

"Okay. The books that don't get on the list go from sixteen to, like, ten thousand, where nobody's counting, right?"

We nodded.

"Okay. So I charge five grand to push a book one spot. If a book is sixteen and not on the list, it's five grand to make it fifteen and on the list. If it's seventeen, it's ten grand to make it fifteen and on the list. Same price to go from three to one, ten grand."

"Is that five thousand per place per week?" Miss Baskerville asked.

"Correct."

"Then some people presumably use your services for more than one week."

"Satisfied customers," Folio said.

"That could be very lucrative."

"Correct," Folio said.

"May I ask you how you got into this operation, Mr. Folio?"

"You may well ask. It started a few years ago when an editor who once worked here left to go into public relations. He was promoting a movie that was being made from a best seller. He called me up. Did I have the names of the bookstores we get our best-seller information from? He'd pay me $500 for it. What did he want it for, I asked. He told me his company had an idea that their movie should come from the number one best seller, and if, for a reasonable amount, they could make it number one, they would. With the names of the bookstores they could send people out and maybe buy enough copies to push it to the top. The book, at the time, was, like, three and not going anywhere. I asked him how much he thought it would take. Ten-fifteen grand, he said—at least that was what the company was willing to spend. I said that even if he did have the names it would be dangerous. Everyone he sent out to buy books would know what was going on. He said if word leaked it would be more publicity, and publicity was publicity. I said that he could never pull the trick again, and he said that's the way it was with great ideas. And I said that, even if he had the names, by the time he got working on it the book would probably be five or lower, and ten-fifteen grand wouldn't be enough. Then I said that for ten-fifteen grand maybe I could arrange to give the book a little push from inside and save everybody sweat and money. And then I added that if everybody was satisfied maybe we could go into business and do it on a regular basis for different companies. He liked the idea, and I said I'd talk it over with the boss, and maybe we could make an arrangement."

"Talk it over with the boss!" Mr. Margin said. "Do these people think I'm party to this fraud?"

"It's hard to tell what people think, Mr. Margin. Maybe they do. I can tell you one thing, they wouldn't be able to understand how the editor didn't know what was going on with his own best-seller lists."

"They're not *my* best-seller lists. It's a mechanical operation. Once it's set up, why should I have anything to do with it?"

"Well, maybe it's more like they wouldn't be able to understand, if there's money around, how the editor wouldn't get some of it. Most of it, in fact. You know, the lion's share to the lion. And there would be no way to prove that the editor didn't. I mean, like, I get five grand a spot. It doesn't show up on my bank statement. Suppose four out of five ended up in your pocket, Mr. Margin, it wouldn't show on your bank statement either. If you see what I mean."

"I see exactly what you mean," Mr. Margin said and looked desperately at Miss Baskerville.

"So if it was up to me, Mr. Margin, I'd swallow the whole thing."

There was a period of silence and common thought. Then Mr. Margin cleared his throat and said, "All right, Folio, I think we have the picture. I suggest you clean out your desk, and I'll call you about the disposition of your case."

"I don't like this, Mr. Margin," Folio said. "I been around here a long time, and I don't think you have the right to throw me out on my can, if you know what I mean."

"What *do* you mean, Folio?"

"I mean, like, I could go to Mr. Tooling. I wouldn't even have to say you were in on the take. I mean, where *were* you, the editor, when I was hustling the review copies and the best-seller list? We'd both be out on our can, Mr. Margin."

There was a thoughtful silence, and Mr. Margin said, "What do you suggest?"

"I been around here a long time, like I said, wrapping bundles, cleaning toilets. I think I deserve something."

"A raise?"

"A promotion, Mr. Margin. I want to be an editor, like everybody else."

"An *editor!*" Mr. Margin said.

"What do you think, Page?" Folio said.

"You certainly seem clever enough."

"That's the way I figure it. So what do you say, Mr. Margin?"

"Leave us, is what I say."

"And you'll let me know."

"We'll let you know," Mr. Margin said in his deepest tones.

As soon as Folio left, Mr. Margin said, "Miss Baskerville, do you think we can keep this among ourselves?"

"Mr. Margin, you may be able to swallow it, but I can't. That man should be in jail. You wouldn't want to conceal a felony, would you?"

"I suppose not," Mr. Margin said.

"Miss Baskerville," I said, "to put Folio away we would have to make the affair public, wouldn't we?"

"Of course."

"Wouldn't it hurt the reputation of the magazine?"

"Perhaps. On the other hand we would be credited with prosecuting a criminal."

"Also," I went on, "don't you think a publishing company whose book didn't become number one because Folio sold the place might want to sue us?"

Mr. Margin sat up at this, and Miss Baskerville fingered her chin. Finally she said that she would discuss the matter with her superiors.

After she left, Mr. Margin thanked me copiously and asked me to talk with Folio. "He likes you. Take him to lunch! See what he really wants!"

I let Folio pick the restuarant, and, sure enough, it was an expensive Mafia hangout, where he was a respected regular. I told him that although I thought he was out of the woods Mr. Margin wasn't. Did he really want to be an editor?

"Babes, I couldn't afford it. I just wanted to give Margin a little thrill. I'm going into a new line of endeavor."

"May I ask what?"

"Can't you guess, with my background in books?"

"A bookie?"

"Correct."

VII

Hit Man

SHORTLY AFTERWARD I WENT ON A TWO-WEEK VACATION, and the Friday before I was to come back Mr. Margin called me in the country to say that he had been replaced.

"By whom?" I said.

"I will tell you this, he is a Protean careerist."

"That doesn't limit the field very much."

"I will also tell you that he has been the editor of more Protean magazines than anyone else."

"You're kidding!"

"I am not kidding," Mr. Margin said.

"What does he know about books?"

"My dear Frank, he has a quality far more valuable."

"You're not going to tell me he knows human nature."

"Not at all. He's *disagreeable.* Colleagues pull their chairs away, look at their laps when he talks, excuse themselves if he goes on too long. Mary Tooling, of course, is transfixed by him."

"Because she's like him?"

"No, no, my dear boy. A corporation doesn't turn up someone so repellent every day. He gets *rid* of people."

It was true. Newbold Press had been hired away from the Rupert Murdoch organization two years before and been moved around from magazine to magazine as a hit man. When Protean forced out the editor of Vin—"the magazine devoted to that spherical miracle known as the grape"—Press was given the job and in three months had gotten rid of a third of the staff, replacing it with cheaper, livelier help. He did the same thing for Moi!—"the magazine for the one person you care most about, You!" In fact, when he was reworking Moi! the staff began rhyming it with *oy.* Soon after, it was announced that Newbold Press would be editor of Esprit—"the magazine that celebrates courage wherever it is found, in man or beast." Instantly and unanimously the staff threatened to quit. Time and Newsweek picked up the story, and Press was withdrawn into the corporate hierarchy, apparently temporarily.

"Can't we do an Esprit?" I said to Mr. Margin.

"I'm afraid not. The whole thing has been accomplished with Hitlerian dispatch. Tool called me to her office the first thing yesterday morning. I was kept waiting—intentionally, it turned out—for one hour. The interview took ten minutes. The burden of her message was not that I *would* be replaced as editor of Belles Lettres but that I *had* been replaced. Newbold Press was, at that very moment, in my—that is, his—office addressing the staff on the new, bold order of things. Tool suggested that I not appear in the office until after the weekend, late Monday afternoon, to be exact, when there will be a party to celebrate Press's appointment as editor of Belles Lettres and my appointment as staff columnist."

"Staff columnist!"

"Didn't you know that it is every editor's dream to be pensioned off with a column? No more administrative detail, no more complaints from readers and advertisers. No more staff problems. No more babies and breakdowns. Just a little reading and writing and drawing one's check."

"How upset are you?"

"I don't know yet, Frank. I suppose I've been expecting it."

"What kind of column?"

"About *books.* What do you think of that for a startling idea? Tool wanted to call it 'The Literary Game.' I said literature was not a game and suggested, ironically, 'Causeries du Lundi.' She agreed, and I thought, why not?"

"But the magazine doesn't come out on Monday."

"We'll be jumping the date. That's good journalism."

"I still don't know why we can't do an Esprit."

"Press has already interviewed the staff, one by one, kicking one half and stroking the other. Virginia, for instance—he asked her what she actually *did* at Belles Lettres. She told me on the phone that when she tried to enumerate her duties her mind went blank. Press kept making remarks like, 'But you must do *something,* Virginia. There are eight hours in the working day. *Think!'* She would say things like, 'I check the captions, I've checked the captions for twenty years.' 'But that takes five minutes, Virginia. How about the rest of the day? Why don't you just go back to your desk and write up a list of the things you do. Take as much time as you need.' She said she hadn't slept all night. So the staff has been divided into those who shall live and those who shall die, to use Tool's phrase. The former, I'm afraid, would not wholeheartedly join a protest, and the latter would have their resignations accepted gladly. Press has done a good job. Of course, it's his specialty."

"Where do I fit in, do you think?"

"He needs you. Tool told me herself. And may I make a suggestion, Frank?"

"Of course."

"Stick it out. He won't last. He's an ignoramus and a vulgarian. The book industry will put pressure on the Toolings to get rid of him. In fact, I don't think he's meant to be there very long."

"Why should I stick around for that?" I said.

"To protect what's left of the staff, Frank."

And I could, I thought. If I gave Press the kind of help he needed I would certainly have some say about the staff.

"Can I help *you,* do you think?" I said.

"Thank you, Frank, but I won't need help. When a corporation has humiliated one of its own, it tends to let him be. It's not that the corporation has a heart, it's that it feels it has implanted a yeasty little lump of self-hatred that will grow and eventually turn the fellow into a crank, at which point everyone will understand why the fellow had to be humiliated in the first place."

"Have they done that to you?"

"We don't know yet, do we?"

"I think I'll stick around," I said.

Newbold Press's thick head of hair was combed half-forward and half-sideways in the manner of Cyrus Tooling Jr., and his face was boyish like a midget's. At my first sight of him, in his office on the following Monday morning, he laid aside a double-breasted blue blazer to reveal a shirt of pale purple with white collar and French cuffs. The blazer, I saw when he put it on at the end of the interview, held a gold watch in the breast pocket, attached by a thong to a crosspiece, passed through the lapel buttonhole. Below the blazer were light gray flannel trousers, gently rolled, and under them shiny gray slip-on shoes with tassels. He spoke in a quacking way and to fill silences rapped his pipe on an ashtray. For the same purpose he coughed and cleared his throat beyond mucose need and made comic noises like "hee-haw" and "hoo-ha." When not making sounds, he filled space with body movement, particularly rubbing his breasts and raising his arms to expose dark patches in the pits. During the interview he got up, walked about a number of times, and lifted his crotch with his hand in the spirit of camaraderie or menace.

What he said was more or less what I had expected, except that I was surprised at his grasp of the characteristics of individual staff members. I also was surprised that he assumed I would be on his side. One remark midway perhaps explained it: "You and I are young, Frank. Protean is middle-aged. The Toolings want me to keep it from getting old. I want you to help me."

When I didn't fill the pause he said, "Do you want to help me?"

"I want to help myself," I said.

Instantly he relaxed. "Ho-*kay*!" he said, pulled his nose, pinkied his ear, and his plans poured forth. "So let's get down to the *meat*. Ellie Bellyband doesn't know the way to the bathroom. What can we do with her? . . . I'm asking you."

"Let me think about it," I said.

"Ho-*kay*!" Ed Princeps should be working on scrolls, not books. Let's take his fifty grand and spread it between two Vassar girls."

I nodded.

"Ho-*kay*!" he said, glancing at his list. "I'm offering Virginia a buy-out. Two years' salary on top of her pension."

"How does she feel about that?"

"She knows she's a pain in the ass and thinks she can hold us up. If she keeps on, she's going to find herself with *nada*. Talk to her!" Press pointed at me in the way, I imagined, I should point at Virginia when I talked to her. "Will you do that?"

"I'll talk to her," I said.

"Ho-*kay*!" And he went on. Chuckle Faircopy, the eccentric who mainly wrote the headlines for Belles Lettres, had to go. "Oversee the headlines," Press said. "Keep rejecting them. Right before we close an issue write your own headlines. Three or four weeks, he'll leave." Lou Bodoni could stay, but she had to quit wearing sweat pants. "I'll take care of that," Press said. Ben Boards, the art director, could stay for now, "but Tool is putting more dough into Belles Lettres. We're not printing on toilet paper anymore. If Boards can keep up with the changes, he can stay. About Margin, I understand he's a friend of yours. Which is fine with me. If you want to take him on, edit his column, keep him happy, be my guest! As for Frank Page, we want to sweeten his pot. He just has to help us. Ho-*kay*?"

I nodded.

He sensed my reserve, because he then said, "Listen, my friend, I don't want to do this job alone. I want help. Who do *you* think should go?"

"Let me think about it," I said.

"Think about it now!"

"It's a serious business, getting rid of someone, serious for the person and serious for the magazine. You want my considered judgment, don't you?"

He looked at me carefully, and I could see that he thought there was a threat in my question, as if I might go to the Toolings and say that Newbold Press had forced me to be precipitate. He didn't say "Ho-*kay*!" He said, "Okay. After lunch. A name."

I phoned Mr. Margin to tell him what had happened. For one thing I thought he might be pleased that I would be handling his copy. He was. Also he was not surprised at anything Press had said.

"How did he have so much information about the staff? You certainly didn't give it to him."

"There's something you should know, Frank," Mr. Margin said, and after a long pause: "There's an informant in the office. I say this with great reluctance. To inform, in my estimation, is worse . . ."

"I don't understand. Someone on the staff reports to . . . whom?"

"Tool. Now Press. This person tried to report to me. I told the person to take the information to higher authority, which I believe the person did. I say this because on more than one occasion Tool knew things about the office she could only have gotten from an informant."

"Like what?"

"One day at a meeting I explained to the staff that if Tool did not like a certain essay I was planning to run on the cover I had another 'at the ready.' Those were my words. Tool did not like the essay, and when I told her I might have trouble filling the spot, she asked if I didn't have another 'at the ready.' Thereafter I barred this person from all sensitive meetings. You may be able to deduce from that who it is."

"I must say, I think you're being an innocent about this, Mr. Margin. There are informers in every office."

He told me the person's name after making me promise never to reveal it and to use the information only to protect myself and the staff. I wasn't surprised. The person was a self-abaser and an obsessive grammarian, to the point of knowing not only right usage but dissenting opinions in the order of their authority. This person never expressed opinions of taste on anything of more consequence than mysteries but applied a natural pedantry with such doggedness that colleagues lost patience. I could see that informing was a way of playing a joke *on* the system *in* the system. It made the person feel better about working below capacity.

"So I guess I'll see you at the party this afternoon," I said.

"Do you think I should prepare a speech?"

"Why not, just in case?" I said.

After lunch I presented the informer's name to Newbold Press as my contribution to his hit list. He thanked me, thoughtfully, I thought.

The party began in the editor's office with the arrival of the Toolings, Mary and Cyrus Jr. Cyrus was a squat man with lumpy skin and lots of hair. Although he was heavy, he had a small voice, small hands, and short arms, which he threw around people for the slightest reason, to commend a piece of work, acknowledge a clever remark, reward extravagant flattery, or just out of bonhomie. As if pulling them close for a photograph, he gathered Press in one arm and Mr. Margin in the other.

"When I think of these two men," he said, beginning his speech, for which everyone quieted down, "I think how aptly my father named this company. Each of them is a Proteus, who, as we know, was a Greek god who could change his shape at will. Marge Margin I can only call a phenomenon. My father hired him fresh out of Harvard. First there was his stint on Homme, which, if I recall, we advertised as 'the magazine that knows where it goes.' Well, it went. The sixties had some ideas about magazines, along with everything else. But, without missing a beat, Marge went as deputy editor to Chez Elle, the only male on the staff. Now *that's*

Protean!" He summoned laughs with a big smile. "And then Belles Lettres, which under Marge's editorship has become the premier literary magazine in the English language."

"Hear, hear!" said Chuckle Faircopy, who was on his third Scotch.

"What more can I say? And now he does still another turn. He's going public, which I truly believe will cover Belles Lettres and himself with glory. I drink to Marge Margin *writer!*"

With this, Cyrus Tooling released Mr. Margin from his grasp and after the polite applause turned to Newbold Press. "My other Proteus is maybe a genius, barely out of his twenties. He has been with me only two years and has edited three magazines before his present assignment. We all know about play doctors—superprofessionals who after the ordinary professionals have done their best come in and sometimes in a matter of hours turn a play from a flop to a hit. . . ."

"Sort of a surgeon," Chuckle said.

"Sometimes a surgeon, yes; sometimes a psychiatrist; sometimes a pediatrician if the patient is young. . . ."

"What is Belles Lettres's disease?" Chuckle said.

"I don't know that Belles Lettres has one," Cyrus Tooling said. "Perhaps an indisposition. Newbold, what would you say was Belles Lettres's indisposition?"

"At the moment," Press said, "loud-mouth complaint."

"I think," Cyrus Tooling said diplomatically, "we'd all like to hear a few words from *Marge Margin!*"

Mr. Margin smiled into his drink, blinked, shook his head as in benign amusement at what he was about to say, sipped his drink, seemed about to speak, then went over to the conference table and turned off the tape recorder that the person he had identified as the informer had brought in to record the proceedings.

"Je parlerai en français," he said, *"puisque nos très importants hôtes ici présents publient Jardin, Théâtre, Mer et Terres. Comme vous avez maintenant un nouveau rédacteur en chef de Belles Lettres, je voudrais parler de lui. Quand il vous demande de faire quelque chose, faites-le immédiatement et sans discuter. Il veut votre obéissance et non pas vos flatteries. S'il veut votre opinion, donnez-la lui, parce qu'il ne s'intéresse pas à ce que vous pensez, mais seulement à ce que vous faites. Ainsi vous conserverez votre amour-propre. Ne montrez pas d'emotion car cet homme est comme un expert de judo, qui retourne contre lui le poids de son adversaire. Enfin, réservez votre dédain pour deux si importants personnages,* Mr. and Mrs. Tooling, who have given over to Newbold Press the premier literary magazine in the English language, Belles Lettres!" Mr. Margin pronounced the last two words ringingly and lifted his glass.

"Bravo!" said Cyrus Tooling.

"Likewise!" said his wife.

VIII

Dead Wood

I WAS SURPRISED TO SEE DAVID LEVINE'S CARICATURE OF Mr. Margin still in the editor's office. Everything else on the walls had changed. I had never paid much attention to Mr. Margin's pictures, but now that they were gone I recalled a number of black-and-white photographs of tree trunks, knotholes, and bark. Now only the Levine remained, which showed a tall, thin, unmistakable Margin standing on one foot on a pile of books, reaching to the top shelf of a high bookcase for a particular volume. The drawing, commissioned by promotion, ran in ads with the line, "For the best go to the top." I know Mr. Margin was pleased with the picture, not only because it hung in his office but because he quoted the line occasionally, along with a modest smile.

Newbold Press saw me looking at the Levine and said, "I asked him to leave it. I told him it was part of the Belles Lettres ambience. . . . And he *left* it," Press added as if he had conned Mr. Margin. "I've told promotion to get a Levine of me. Got any ideas?"

"For a Levine of you?" I thought of a semi-simian figure holding a pipe in one hand and looking at a book upside down in the other. What I said to him was, "How about a figure holding a pipe like yours, but very big, and around the bowl are carved famous literary names, like around a library?"

"Like what names?"

"The usual."

"For instance."

"Hesiod, Homer, Pindar, Pattia, Maxina, Laverna. . . . You get the idea."

After a serious pause he said, "Send me a memo on the names."

"There'd only be room for three or four."

"A *memo*!"

"Will do."

"Ho-*kay*!" he said. "Now down to business. I have Faircopy's headlines. Rewrite them, but show them to me before you show them to him."

"I tell him you didn't like them, right?"

"Wrong. You tell him *you* didn't like them."

"Maybe I will like them."

"You don't understand," Press said. "I've not only decided these heads are bad, I've decided that *you've* decided they're bad."

We looked at one another for a few seconds, he with the

fixed smile he had learned from Mrs. Tooling. Without comment I held out my hand for the headlines. Without comment he gave them to me.

That evening I phoned Mr. Margin to see how his first column was going. It was due the next day.

"I thought I'd do two things, Frank. First, introduce myself, so to speak. I am, after all, anonymous to most readers. Then talk about the frustrations an editor feels at having to communicate through the words of others, as against the sense of power and freedom he feels at the opportunity to speak directly. . . ."

"Is that how you feel, powerful and free?"

"Frank, I feel weak and constrained. I'm not a writer. I discovered that years ago."

"Then you can't write about feeling powerful and free. Why not explain what a magazine editor really does, guides a company of writers the way a conductor guides a company of musicians, trying to make them do more together than they could apart. Isn't that what you did?"

"That's what I felt I did."

"So why not explain it. People would be interested."

"I'll try it."

"And may I make a suggestion?"

"Of course."

"Write it fast. You may not be a writer, but you're a talker. Talk into the typewriter. It's only eight hundred words. Call me when it's done."

He called back in an hour, read me the column, and it was okay.

Then I rewrote Chuckle Faircopy's headlines. A few of them would have fallen by the wayside anyhow. On facing pages, for instance, were matched reviews, one of a volume of Shaw's letters, the other of a selection of George Eliot's letters. Faircopy had written matched (to say the least) heads: "Sincerely, George" and "Sincerely, George." I changed them to "Man of Letters" and "Woman of Letters." Most of the other heads were perfectly okay, and one of them, for a book about the making of Michael Cimino's film "Heaven's Gate," was perfectly perfect—"Epic Failure." I let it be.

The next morning Press looked them over and said, "Change 'Epic Failure' to 'Failure of an Epic'!"

"We lose the play," I said.

"We don't like the play," he said. "Change it and show him what you did!"

I put off seeing Faircopy as long as I could, but production would soon be asking for heads, so right before noon I went to his desk. He was already at work on next week's issue.

"Chuckle," I said, "the heads."

"Shoot!" He waved me into his visitor's chair, where I sat while he studied the changes.

He took a long time. Finally he said, "This is the work of a prick."

"Chuckle . . ."

"You're not the prick, Frank. I can figure out what's going on."

"Are you sure?"

"I'll tell you how sure I am. For next week I'll do two sets of heads, a real one and a false one. I'll give the real one to you and the false one to the prick. Then when you rewrite them you can use the real one. Are you game?"

"I am."

"I would never mistake you for a prick, Frank. Not that kind."

"Thanks," I said and felt as you do when somebody's pet likes you.

After lunch Press called me into his office. He held up Mr. Margin's copy. "What do you two think you're doing?"

"In what way?"

"Have you read this?"

"No," I said, which was true.

"He's writing about being the editor. I'm the editor. He's a columnist. Was this your idea?"

"I haven't even read the column," I said.

"Get him on the phone and tell him it's no good."

"May I tell him *you* don't like it?"

"You bet your sweet ass you can."

As ordered, I called Mr. Margin, but what I said was, "Will you do something without asking why?"

After a pause he said, "Of course, Frank."

"Do you have a carbon of your column?"

"Yes."

"Bring it to the building and show it to Mr. Tooling. Just say you want his opinion."

"Why, Frank?"

"Trust me. He'll be flattered. Will you do it?"

"If you think I should."

"Call me right away and tell me what he says."

* * *

In fifteen minutes Press was at my desk. "Did you get him?"

"He's not in," I said, which was probably true.

"Keep after him! Let me know when you get him!"

"Ho-*kay*!" I said.

In forty-five minutes Mr. Margin called down from the publisher's office. His column was a great success. "Cyrus actually said if he had known I wrote so well he would have made the change years ago. Also, he said he was *flattered.*"

"Congratulations."

"Thank you, Frank."

"Did you get him?" Press said as I came into his office.

"He called me to say that Mr. Tooling liked his column."

"He showed it to Tooling?"

"Apparently."

"And Tooling said what?"

"He liked it."

"Did you tell Margin I didn't like it?"

"I thought I'd better see you first."

"Okay, let's forget it. Put the column through!"

I turned to go.

"Let him know that one piece on the subject is plenty."

"He probably understands that. He was an editor himself."

I phoned Mr. Margin that evening and related everything that had happened.

"You're a clever young man," he said. "However, Press may see what you're up to. Be careful."

The next morning Press asked me to have lunch with him. "Make reservations at your favorite restaurant! It's on Protean."

I made them at my second favorite, not wanting to contaminate the first.

Would he stroke me, threaten me, call on my sense of common purpose? None of these. He explained himself. After a few of what passed with him for pleasantries he spoke a paragraph: "Let me introduce myself. I am a man who at the precocious age of thirteen experienced an astonishing revelation: It is better to be a success than a failure. Money, I saw, was important: It is better to be rich than to be poor. Power, I saw, was desirable: It was better to give orders than to take them. Fame, I saw, was delicious: It was better to be recognized than to be anonymous. You agree with that?"

I hardly knew what to say. He was quoting from something, and I didn't know what it was, nor have I been able to find out since.

He repeated: "You agree with that?"

I said I probably did, although it seemed to me it mattered what one had to do to attain these things. I added that I didn't think everyone else would agree with it.

"I'm not talking losers."

"Neither am I," I said.

He went on to say he had been a bright boy in grade school. His teachers pleaded with his father to send him to a special high school. "He sent me to a special school all right.

I learned to be an auto mechanic. I can take a car apart with my feet." He had to work his way through college, although his father could well have afforded to send him. He didn't tell me how he had broken into the editorial business. It wasn't clear to me, either, how he felt about himself. Had he triumphed over his father, had he disobeyed him?

Also, I didn't know how he wanted me to feel about him. Was I supposed to be sorry for him, admiring of him? Or was this just neutral information? At any rate, his story seemed to call for some kind of reciprocation, and I searched my memory for an instance of parental betrayal. The best I could come up with was my appendectomy. My mother had told me I was just going into the hospital for an examination.

"That really scarred me," I added.

When I was leaving that evening I ran into Tool on the elevator. She looked me over with her black eyes and said, "You had lunch with Newbold today."

I allowed as I had.

"You like him better now?" she said.

"Better than what?"

"Better than before."

I thought about it, and, since I hadn't liked him at all before, I said, honestly, "Much."

Tool nodded, confirming her own wisdom.

What had she said to him? You're a nice boy, Newbold. Tell him about yourself. He'll like you.

Next morning Press was all business again. I should get on with the housecleaning and persuade Virginia Wrappers to retire. I asked him why he wasn't using on her the same heavy hand he was using on the others.

"Don't you know about The Buckram Curse?" he said and explained that when Aubrey Buckram sold Belles Lettres to Cyrus Tooling Sr. it was stipulated that no staffer could be fired out of hand. If Tooling wanted to get rid of someone he'd have to pay the person off. Including Virginia, there were only seven on the staff at the time. Still, the clause was a challenge to Tooling. He considered selling Belles Lettres and buying it back, judging, probably correctly, that The Buckram Curse would disappear in the process. Then a simpler device occurred to him. One by one he persuaded three of the seven staffers to move to other Protean magazines. Six months after each one made the switch the person was fired with two weeks' severance. The first two took it lying down. The second, in fact, committed suicide. The third, however, threatened to sue. Cyrus's lawyers advised that such a suit would have no merit, but his publicity department pointed out that The Village Voice would be sure to write it up. Also, Protean at the time was fighting an attempt to unionize the company; and the story, if it got out, wouldn't help much. All in all, it might be better to reinstate the man. The man, however, didn't want reinstatement; he wanted to sue, for mental anguish and injury to his professional reputation. "That baby," Press said, "walked away with a bundle."

I said I didn't really know what he wanted me to do with Virginia. "I can't negotiate with her, I don't know what you're offering."

"Just find out what's on her mind," Press said.

"Such as it is," I said.

* * *

At lunch the next day Virginia sidestepped my approaches to the subject of a buy-out, and when I actually asked her if she had been offered one she said things like, "You know how they are here. Talk, talk, talk." When I indicated that perhaps I could be of some help with such talk she narrowed her eyes and merely said, "Perhaps." She also surprised me by expressing admiration for Press and the changes he was making. "He certainly has a brilliant record. Can you imagine, all those jobs, at *his* age! Just discussing possibilities with Newbold has set my mind a-racing. I haven't had so many ideas in years and years."

I didn't know what to make of it. She herself had said to me a week before that three minutes with Press was like thirty minutes on the subway. Then it occurred to me that she must have thought I was representing Press and would report back her compliments.

Luckily Virginia liked a glass of wine with her meals. After the second she admitted that she *had* been offered a buy-out by Press, but probably I didn't know why: Mr. Tooling was considering her for Press's job.

I expressed mild surprise at this and asked her as gently as I could how she had come by the news. She said she was not at liberty to say, but it was from an unimpeachable source, "very near the top."

"Well, how do you feel about this, Virginia? Do you want the job?"

"Not for myself," she said, "for American letters." On the other hand, there were younger people than she around; on still another hand, how many were there with her experience?

"I would want you to continue as my assistant editor," she said, "assuming you are willing to serve, Frank."

I indicated as best I could that I would be willing.

"How soon, Virginia, do you think such a change might take place?"

"I am not at liberty to say. I *can* say, though, sooner rather than later."

I nodded knowingly, and she smiled in the same spirit. To overcome my own silence I asked if we should have another wine to celebrate. She agreed, adding coyly, "We must always remember there's many a slip twixt the cup and the lip."

"Let's hope not in this case," I said. "And, Virginia, may I make a suggestion? If Press offers you a job on another Protean magazine promise me you'll turn it down."

Again she narrowed her eyes. Whether she was recalling what had happened years before to the people who had changed jobs or whether she was contemplating an even greater destiny for herself I couldn't tell. What she said was, "Cold, I'll turn it down cold."

Later in the afternoon Press asked me how I had done with Virginia and how it was going generally with the dead wood. I nodded diagonally, which is to say philosophically.

"The trouble with you, Page, is you have no taste for blood."

IX

Good Meeting

In a tradition that went back as far as anyone could remember, assignment meetings were held in the editor's office on Monday afternoons. Everyone was eager to see how Press would handle them.

He was away for the first three and had left me in charge. The proceedings were so familiar they ran themselves. The only thing I did was resist jokes about Press, which, once begun, would have reduced business to giggles. For instance, Ed Princeps, after recommending for review a history of the changing attitudes toward baldness, wondered if we shouldn't wait for New*bald*'s presence to pick a reviewer. Barry Vellum said we should have the new balls to make up our own minds.

Lou Bodoni objected to the use of male parts to signify courage. Someone said we should press on, and Virginia Wrappers asked us all to speak up. I proposed that we give the book to Mr. Margin, who was preparing tailpieces on literary curiosities for his column.

As Press's first meeting approached he showed his nervousness by sending around an unnecessary memo to the effect that there would *be* a meeting. The memo directed that it itself be passed from desk to desk, initialed, and returned to Press. Along the way it picked up the rhetorical initials "P.U.," "F.U.," and "B.S." as well as legitimate initials. I intercepted it, went to Press's office, and announced that everyone had seen it.

I suggested to Press that perhaps I ought to continue to run the meetings until he got the hang of it, but he said, "No. What you *can* do is be my Ed McMahon."

"You mean, 'Heeere's Newbold!'?"

"You got it."

I thought, of course, this was banter. But on Monday afternoon, when the staff was seated and settled, Press nodded to me. I nodded back. He raised his eyebrows and nodded again, and I said, "Heeere's Newbold!"

The staff was shocked, thinking I was being insubordinate. But Press picked it right up: "I can see you're a good group. Let's keep the laughing down. The engineers tell me we can be heard in the next studio. One of the vice-presidents is taping a sermonette." He waited, and when there was no response he said, "Ho-*kay*! Today we'll be hearing about the mysterious B. Traven. We have a proposal from the inimitable Lewis Auchincloss. We're going to match the two leading heavyweights, Saul Bellow and John Irving, in the battle of the decade. And much, much more."

The editor's large, ornate desk had become part of Belles Lettres's furniture during Xavier Deckle's days. Press now sat behind it on a handsome swivel chair that, unknown to him, could be raised and lowered like a piano stool. Since Mr. Margin was a tall man the seat was wound down, and now the desk came up to Press's breastbone. With his elbows out and leaning forward he looked like a hungry turtle.

"First, B. Traven. I have here in my hot little hand a letter from a man in Santa Fe who claims to know the identity of B. Traven and is ready, willing, and able to reveal it." Press looked around the room. "Any comment?"

No comment.

"Who's the Traven maven here? Ed, how about you?"

"It is generally agreed," Ed Princeps said, "that B. Traven was the pseudonym of Berick Traven Torsvan. One theory has it that he was born in Chicago in 1890, another that he was a native of Germany. It seems clear that he was active in the IWW and lived in Mexico from the twenties until his death in 1969."

"A-plus! So you're saying we shouldn't do it."

"I didn't say that."

"What did you say?"

"Only what I said."

"All right, what's your opinion?"

"I have no opinion."

"Force yourself!" Press said.

Ed opened a book and began to read.

Barry Vellum said, "Why don't we print what Ed just said and let it go at that?"

"When I want *your* opinion I'll ask for it," Press said.

"Newbold," I said, "why don't we tell the man in Santa Fe to give us more details and we'll decide when we hear from him."

"Do it!" Press said and held the letter out in such a way that I had to get up to take it from him.

"Ho-*kay*!" Press picked up another letter and said, "Lewis Auchincloss wants to write an appreciation of Gore Vidal. What do you think . . . Virginia?"

"Didn't Gore Vidal do an appreciation of him in The New York Review?" she said.

"That was *Louis* Auchincloss," Chuckle Faircopy said.

I was watching Press. It was hard to tell how much he understood of what was going on. At any rate, he dropped the idea and took up his heavyweights.

"Tool and I want to get the two biggies, John and Saul, in the ring. Put them together with a mike and a referee and let them go. We'll print it all, the grunts, the groans, the squeals, as well as the pearls of wisdom. I'm not asking if this is a good idea—it *is*—I'm asking what they should talk about."

"May I say something please?" Barry Vellum said.

Press nodded.

"What makes you think they'd be so fierce?"

"We're talking egos, we're talking king of the hill, we're talking big time. Maybe it should be, Whose characters are better? Whose plots are better?"

"Whose is bigger, yours or mine?" Barry said.

"You got it."

"Maybe," I said, "if they haven't agreed yet, we should see first if they're willing and then ask what they'd like to talk about, or fight about."

"Do it!" Press said to me. Then to the secretary: "Selma, after the meeting get Irving and Bellow on the phone and put them through to Frank."

"Which one first?" she said.

"Whoever comes through first," Press said.

Since Rose Cloth's departure we had been doing with temporary help from Protean's floating pool. By the time Press arrived we had a young woman reasonably familiar with books. Mr. Margin had intended to hire her permanently but hadn't gotten around to it. I suggested to Press that he hire her, but after three days he requested a replacement and now had Selma Watermark, who was a serious middle-aged woman and the only person in the office Press was polite to. I thought at first it might be because she reminded him of his mother or an aunt, then I realized it was because she was the only one who knew less about books than he did.

"Ho-*kay*! Let's do *books*! It's all yours, Frankie boy."

As always Ed Princeps had the largest pile, and I nodded to him. He started in not only without his usual introductory pleasantries, he affected a suspiciously businesslike air: "I have in front of me a very ambitious, very imaginary first novel concerning a Roman Catholic adolescent who undergoes a crisis of faith. Try as he may he cannot accept the doctrine of transubstantiation, which as we know teaches that bread and wine when consecrated become the body and blood of Christ. He wants to give the doctrine every chance. So one day at mass after receiving communion he removes the host from his mouth and secretes it in a handkerchief. He takes the host home and dries it out. Then for many pages of rich, bravura writing the hero contemplates the host lying before him on his desk. It begins to glow, to move, to make sounds. . . ."

The galley proofs in Ed's hand were not, I could see, a first novel at all but a new book by Larry McMurtry. So I said, "Maybe, Ed, instead of the plot we ought to get on with the assignment. I gather you feel the book should be reviewed."

"Absolutely, and I have the perfect reviewer. John Bark."

Press said, "Why?"

"Well, as author of 'The Fot-Seed Wactor' he is unarguably the one man capable of dealing with this ingenious work."

Press said, "What do you think, Frank?"

Before I could answer, Chuckle Faircopy said, "May I make another suggestion? This is obviously a novel of some religious import, and although I defer to no one in my admiration for John Bark, perhaps we should think of using his brother, the theologian Karl Bark."

"He's dead," Virginia Wrappers said.

"Well, that answers that," Press said. "You got it all, Selma?"

"How do I spell it?" she said.

I leaned over and said that she and I would review things later.

The rest of the meeting was not uneventful. Among the other assignments it was agreed to send a chocolate cookbook to John Hershey, a book of literary criticism to Calvin Trilling, a book on entomology to Gregor Samsa, and a feminist novel to Doris Grumble. There was one point at which I thought we were in trouble. Press introduced the name of the publisher Alfred A. Knopf, and Lou Bodoni, who to my surprise got into the act, kept referring to Alfred Nopf until Press changed his pronunciation.

After the others left, Press said to me that I had to admit he gave good meeting. I agreed and said I thought the staff gave good meeting too.

I was hardly back in my office when Press showed up, pink with confidence. "Let's make the rounds," he said.

"The rounds?"

"Let's kick a little ass. And bring your clipboard!"

The clipboard, I soon saw, had no function but to put me into an attendant relation to Press.

He began with Ellie Bellyband, who always seemed to have a half-eaten cupcake on her desk. And, sure enough, as we approached, her stockinged feet were propped on an upended wastebasket, and she was licking her fingers. She had gotten to the middle finger.

"I want you to feel at home here," Press said, "and I don't want you to go hungry. A little nibble is good for the brain cells. But if you have to eat between meals Mr. Tooling has provided a cafeteria. You wouldn't want Mr. Tooling to get mice here, would you?"

Ellie put her feet on the floor, sat up straight, and looked at Press with a mixture of surprise and sullenness.

"Don't people answer questions around here?"

"What's the question?" Ellie said.

"Do you want Mr. Tooling to get mice?"

"I thought that was a rhetorical question."

"It wasn't."

I watched a variety of responses play over Ellie's face. Finally she said, "No."

Next we moved to Ben Boards, the art director, who sat on a high stool at a long table that was almost entirely covered with graphics debris. In a small clearing he was turning over old Dick Tracy tearsheets. He was so used to Mr. Margin's tolerance of his outside activities that he didn't think to put the comic strips aside.

"What's up, chief?"

"What's up is that I'd like a day's work for a day's pay."

Ben had many interests. He produced as editor or packager perhaps five books a year, as well as mounting occasional art shows for corporations and universities. He always seemed to get his Protean work done, however. He now asked Press what his beef was.

"I understand that you don't have enough to do around here. From now on when you think you're done just keep working and make it better. Also you can take the dreck on this table that doesn't belong to Belles Lettres and get rid of it. If that doesn't suit you I'll ask Mr. Tooling to charge you rent. You get me?"

Ben said nothing.

"You get me?"

Ben pursed his lips ironically and nodded.

"I want to *hear* it," Press shouted.

"Yes," Ben shouted back.

I could see there was no order to Press's progress. He went to whatever caught his eye. Next we advanced on Belles Lettres's new copyboy, Bobby Quarto, a young man who had taken a term off from Princeton "to look around," as he put it. He was lanky and fair and addressed older males as "sir," which for myself I found mildly irritating. At the moment he was addressing the pretty, black copygirl from Voilà ("the magazine with a passion for fashion"), whose offices were across the hall.

He received Press and me with a boyish smile. I think he thought he was about to impress the girl by the social ease with which he handled the boss.

"Hi, sir!" he said.

"Sniff pussy on your own time," Press said.

"Sir?"

Press repeated it, and Bobby drew him forward by his tie. "We don't talk that way in front of ladies, do we, sir?"

Press said nothing. I don't think he could.

"Do we, sir?"

Press shook his head. Bobby released him, and he fell back. I let him return to his office by himself.

"No offense to you, sir."

"Okay, but I'd say you don't have much of a future here. In fact, maybe you'd better . . ."

"Yes, sir," he said and produced from the kneehole of his desk a ready carryall to take his things away.

"And you," I said to the girl, "better go back to your office." She instantly disappeared.

Only one other staff member saw what had happened, but

it sped around the office and accounted, I think, for what came next.

Near the end of the afternoon I noticed that most of the staff were not at their desks. Eventually they wandered back, and then, just before closing, the office informer phoned me (although the informer wasn't twenty yards away) to ask if we could meet at a nearby bar.

If I were choosing an informer for a movie I wouldn't pick this one, who was a perfect cliché: deferential crouch, nervous eyes, shameful smile, wet lips. I had a feeling that any quick movement on my part and this person would duck, fearful of being hit.

The informer told me that the staff had gathered in a Protean conference room and voted unanimously to take action against Press. Among the proposals were a letter of protest to the publisher, a public statement at the forthcoming stockholders' meeting, a thinly disguised satire about Press to be published in some magazine like The Nation. It was also recalled that Art Folio had once boasted that he could have anyone rubbed out for $500 to $750, depending on how well known the party was. Several contributions were immediately pledged. Ed Princeps, who more or less chaired the meeting, said a "de-Press-ion" committee would be formed to consider alternatives and that nothing would be done without the approval of the majority of the staff.

I asked the informer if he (or she) would be on the committee. Yes.

I also asked if there had been any discussion of security. Yes, my name had come up. Chuckle Faircopy said he would vouch for my goodwill. On the other hand, Ellie Bellyband said I had shown my true colors by joining Press on his afternoon tour. Ed Princeps said he fully agreed with Chuckle, but since my position on Belles Lettres was ambiguous, being between staff and management, my presence at the meeting would have compromised me.

Finally I said to the informer, "How come you're telling me this rather than telling Press?" and the informer said, "Because I trust you, Frank."

What kind of reverse projection was that, I wondered.

In the evening I phoned Ed Princeps and told him about the informer, whom he must get off the committee. Ed thought for a while, then said he would convene the committee without the informer, after which he would hold another, false meeting with the informer.

I also phoned Mr. Margin to tell him the day's happenings. He said I should realize that the informer had certainly told Press first and Press had told the informer to tell me. "Press is testing you. You must go to him first thing in the morning and tell him everything, like a genuine helpmeet."

The best I could do was say to Press, "You heard about it, of course."

"About what?"

"It."

He studied me, dug in his nose as if for wisdom, and said, "Yeah, I know about it. How did you know I know about it?"

"Don't you think I'm clever enough to have figured it out?"

"Maybe."

He was right. I wouldn't have figured it out by myself.

"Anyway," Press said, leaning forward in his hungry-turtle mode, "this is my meat. I'll pick them off one by one."

X

Cold Shoulder

I GOT NO MORE INFORMATION FROM THE INFORMER, BUT I did get some from Ed Princeps. He called me at home to say the real meeting had been held at his apartment, with Barry Vellum, Lou Bodoni, and Chuckle Faircopy.

And:

(1) None of them was surprised by the fact or identity of the informer; they all distrusted solitaries.

(2) They decided a letter to the publisher was no good now. Knowing about it, Press would have explained it away.

(3) Barry suggested that he "get friendly" with Selma ("I'll sacrifice myself") and see what could be learned about Press's expense account. Lou Bodoni asked why this was a man's job;

she could "approach Selma socially" with the same results. Lou got the job.

(4) Lou said that she had observed Press mailing his personal letters, which meant that he kept his own supply of stamps. How about treating the backs with LSD? "We get medical over, and they take him away with what looks like a nervous breakdown." Ed pointed out that this would be a criminal offense, and the idea was dropped.

(5) Chuckle said he was working on something but preferred not to talk about it now.

(6) Ed suggested that everyone keep a log of Press's particularly ignorant and abusive remarks. Barry said he had heard Press refer to "'Lady Chatterly's Lover' by Lawrence of Arabia." Nobody believed him (but I had heard it too).

I asked Ed if they had had the false meeting.

"We're having it tomorrow night here at my place, but we've planned it. No one will be able to agree. Then Lou will call Barry a pig and leave in a huff."

"That's not enough, Ed. Press is no fool. A real meeting wouldn't go like that."

"How would it go?"

"It would go like the real meeting you had. In fact you could repeat that meeting. Those ideas are harmless."

"Do *you* have any ideas?"

"Let me talk with Mr. Margin. He sees things from a different angle."

Mr. Margin was interested in the LSD, not as a plan but as a concept. He said that when you're in charge of people, especially when you're responsible for firing, promoting, giving and withholding raises, you have a sense that anyone might do anything to you. "Like an officer leading men into battle. That fellow you refused the weekend pass to, he could shoot you in the back with complete impunity. By the way, whose idea was the LSD?" I told him. "Yes, Lou especially. Did you know she carries a penknife? She sharpens pencils with it, although there's a perfectly good electric sharpener in the office. She used to take it out and play with it at production meetings. Once she opened it and cleaned her fingernails. I asked her after the meeting not to do that anymore. She asked if I found it threatening."

"What did you say?"

"I said there's a time and place for one's toilet. Do you know what she said? She said, 'I do other things in my toilet.' No, I tell you, Frank, if I were Press I'd keep my stamps in my wallet."

So much for Mr. Margin's contribution.

Ed reported on the false meeting. What sounded like a good idea came from, of all people, the informer: The staff should play on Press's nerves—no one go into his office unless bidden, no one initiate a conversation with him, everyone respond to his questions and directions in the shortest way.

"You realize," I said, "Press would know about it beforehand."

"He'd catch on right away anyhow. That wouldn't make it any the less unsettling. But what do you think about where the idea came from?"

"I think we're dealing with a double agent of sorts," I said.

"What do you mean?"

"If you were the informer wouldn't you want to create diversions for yourself?"

Ed agreed he would.

Press called me into his office the next morning as soon as I arrived. "What do you know about Operation Cold Shoulder?"

"I never heard of it." Actually I had not heard the name.

He studied me in what I think he thought was a piercing manner, then said, "That gang out there is going to ignore me."

"Ignore you?"

"Ignore me, ignore me. You understand English?"

"Yes," I said, not wanting to get caught in one of his routines.

"There's a reason those meatballs are out there and I'm in here. What do they think, they're going to break my heart by not talking to me? I could give them something that would really do it."

"Like what?"

"Like if each of them slipped five mistakes into every issue, I'd be out in a month. . . ." He cut himself short. And indeed it was a good idea. "You want to see something? . . . Selma, tell Virginia Wrappers to get in here! . . . Watch this!"

Virginia entered as if marching, fists clenched, lips sealed.

Press came around from his desk, pulled out a chair, and

held it for her. "Take a load off your feet, Virginia!" She sat down and gave me a hard look. She didn't know my position, and probably just as well.

Press took out another chair for himself, so we were a triangle. "I just want to tell you, Virginia, that I've been reviewing your work, and I've misjudged you. I want to apologize if I've been rough on you. I'm new here, and I can't see everything at once. I want you to know that for me you represent *class* in this magazine. I was listening to you at the meeting the other day, and I really heard what you were saying. So I want to give you a chance to tell me *personally* what we should do with the magazine." He sat back with an encouraging smile, and her ideas poured out.

She recommended a different format for page one, reviewers we hadn't used in a long time (some because they were dead), a change of typeface, an abbreviated best-seller list, a quotation-finding service for readers. I was surprised at the extent as well as the consistency of the suggestions. Then I realized she was describing the Belles Lettres put out by Xavier Deckle when she joined the magazine.

"Well, Virginia, I'm impressed," he said, and he was.

"Thank you, Newbold. The worst thing in the world is to work hard and not be appreciated. Mr. Deckle appreciated me. Mr. Backstrip appreciated me. Even Skippy Overleaf appreciated me. And Mr. Margin said exactly what you said, that I was Belles Lettres's conscience. In fact, he said I was 'our avatar of taste.'"

The burden of the rest of her message was that books had been her life, that if she could make even a small contribution to literature her place on earth would be justified, that although not all of us can be poets or novelists we should accept the responsibilities of our lesser station with dignity and prosecute them with diligence.

After this, Press rose to signify the end of the interview. "Keep up the good work, Virginia, and watch for a little something in your next paycheck."

"Thank you, Newbold," she said and left dabbing at an eye with a tissue.

"See what I mean?" Press said.

I thought of asking him if he could do it with the rest of the staff but didn't. Maybe he could.

Before I left he told me to have everyone in his office at 2:30.

At 2:25 the staff was assembled outside Press's office. The door was closed. No one had seen him come back from lunch, but apparently he had; Selma assured us he was in there. Then at 2:30 he opened the door. We filed in and arranged ourselves on chairs, along the window seat, a few against the wall. We all faced Press, who sat behind his desk looking pleased with himself.

The staff looked pleased too, in a determined way. I think they were expecting a test of wills—Press would badger them, they would remain silent.

"Ho-*kay*! Today we have a big treat. And lucky for you, you won't have to say a word." He picked up what looked like a napkin and read from it: "'You all know his work, you all know his life. Both have been an open book. He has been called many things. Boor, bully, bum. He's also been called America's genius. He prefers the last, but he sees the point of the others. He's been known to help an old lady across the street and smack a young one in the chops. He once invited the wife of an American president to go to bed with him, and he thinks she should have—he got her husband the job. People say he's soft on murderers, and maybe he is, having looked into his heart and seen murder there more than once. So I give you *numero uno,* the man who talks turkey and not only on Thanksgiving.'"

Press held out his hand, palm up, toward the clothes closet. When nothing happened he said again, louder, "'. . . and not only on Thanksgiving.'" When still nothing happened he got up and opened the closet door. There in profile was a well-known American writer, a drink in one hand, his penis in the other, urinating on Press's coat. Chuckle Faircopy broke into applause. The rest of the staff followed. Even Press joined in. The writer shook himself off, zipped up, and stepped into the room.

"Thank you," he said. "I wrote that finely balanced introduction myself. But there was more to it: 'I give you a man who knows a woman's place in the world and a man's place in a woman.' Newbold, why did you leave that out?"

Lou Bodoni booed.

"That's why," Press said, maneuvering the writer into a chair. "But you promised at lunch to tell us what you think of Belles Lettres."

"Fantastic."

"What do you like best?"

"The words and pictures."

"Is there any way we can improve it?"

"None."

"Then you think it's perfect."

"Perfect," the writer said and took a sip of his drink, which looked like straight Scotch or bourbon. "I'm more interested in you, Newbold. I like you. You're such an ugly little brute. Did you know you have an animal face. One of those dodgy little animals. A mole. Burrows, eats bugs, tough muzzle, silky light-brown fur, forefeet good for digging. You must have been one repulsive kid, Newbold. So why fight it? Everyone thinks you're a creep, you'll be a creep. You know why I like you, Newbold? You have no pride. You're a prince of the possible."

Press smiled through this.

But when Chuckle called out, "Hear, hear!" the writer said, looking vaguely in Chuckle's direction, "Let me tell you something, flunkie. It's all right for me to dump on Newbold. I'm a celebrity, and he enjoys it. But you're one of his creatures. You don't have the right to say anything but 'Yes, sir!' "

"Hear, hear!" Press said.

"Never take your eye off the help, Newbold, they'll steal you blind." He turned to the staff. "As I look out on this sea of mediocrity I want to pull the plug and let you drain away. You call yourself adults? Why do you stay under the heel of this little thug? He'd stomp you bloody for a two-bit bonus. The big thugs are bad enough, but the little ones! They abuse you not only because it's good for them, they enjoy it. They're free-will fascists, and you are their volunteers. Go get a job over people dumber and weaker than you and you can be free-will fascists too."

"Are you a free-will fascist?" Barry Vellum called out.

"You bet. My publisher sends me birthday presents, get-well cards, tells me all the good things people say about me at parties. You know why? If he didn't I'd get a new publisher. I won't tell you what his female assistant does for me."

Barry got to his feet. "Are you saying there are two classes of people, the exploiters and the exploited?"

"That man needs a drink," the writer said.

"Do you remember me?" Barry went on. "We shared a room at college."

"Honey, I see three of you, and I don't remember any one of them. I'm getting sick of this, Newbold. Let's get out of here."

Press got the writer's coat. I helped the writer to his feet. He had stopped performing, his eyes were half-closed, and his jaw was working in what looked like one kind of nausea or another.

As Press held the coat he said to me, "Some show!"

Near the end of the week I reported all this to Mr. Margin, adding that it seemed to me Operation Cold Shoulder had been a failure. The problem was that it hadn't changed anything. Nobody wanted to talk to Press anyhow. He had been getting the cold shoulder from the start. Mr. Margin said he thought the visiting writer had been very perceptive, Press really had no pride. "The point of ostracism, after all, is moral disdain. That fellow couldn't care less. Frank, maybe you should all relax and accept him like bad weather."

The next day, Friday, Selma came into my office after lunch and said that Press was acting funny, would I come look?

He was slumped in his chair, chin on chest, hands on his desk like paws. He was sweating, slavering, breathing hard, and was very pale. I asked him if he was all right, and he struck at something in front of his face, like a fly or a cobweb. Selma asked if she could help. He retched, and one eye blinked like a flickering light. I told Selma to call medical and wait outside till they came.

A male nurse arrived with a wheelchair. Press was inert. The male nurse wiped his forehead, felt it, took his pulse, and asked him how he was doing.

"Get me away from the wall!" Press said.

"What wall, fella?"

"He's afraid the books will fall on him," I said.

"What's this, fella?" The male nurse held up a finger.

Press covered his eyes.

"Look, it's a lolly."

Press peeked through his fingers and smiled.

"Okay, fella, upsy-daisy!"

We lifted him into the wheelchair.

"Acid?" I asked.

"Something like that. We'll bring him down, then you can send someone around and take him home. What's with him tripping in the office?"

"I guess the pressure of the job."

"I know what you mean," the male nurse said.

Everyone noticed Press being wheeled to the elevator. Word went around that he had had a heart attack, an epileptic fit, a generous thought. I removed the stamps from Press's desk and told Ed Princeps what had happened. He said he'd talk to Lou Bodoni.

XI

Letters to the Editor

PRESS WAS BACK ON MONDAY CONVINCED HE HAD HAD food poisoning. He called me into his office. "Drop everything!" he said. "I want you to send a letter to the ten best critics in America and ask them what they think of the new Belles Lettres."

"What new Belles Lettres?" I said.

"Since I took over."

"I haven't noticed anything new."

"You're too close to it. I want to find out what people think, especially critics. Okay?"

"Let me get this straight. I pick ten critics . . ."

"The ten *best* critics."

"There aren't ten good critics around," I said.

"So? The least worst. You get the idea."

"I pick the ten least worst critics in America. I send them a letter. All the same letter?" Press nodded. "Which asks what they think of the 'new' Belles Lettres. Do I tell them it's new or do they know it?"

"Just say the 'new Belles Lettres'! What's the matter with you, Page? This isn't complicated."

"What is it for?"

"It's for me. It's for my information."

"Under whose name does the letter go out?"

"Yours. You write the letter, you sign it."

"Suppose I don't write it, do I have to sign it?"

"Page, I can get someone else to do this."

"Why don't you," I said and started to get up.

Press pointed at me. "Because I want *you* to do it."

I considered refusing and quitting, and refusing and getting fired, but I said, "Okay."

"Ho-*kay*! Show me the letter tomorrow and the list of critics. Selma will get it out."

The letter, which should have been easy, was agony. Mainly, I think, because I didn't know what Press was up to. After many long and short versions I ended at midnight at home, full of Scotch, with: "The new editor of Belles Lettres, Newbold Press, would like to know what you think of the new Belles Lettres. Thank you." I must have been quite drunk because it seemed perfect when I went to bed.

"What's this," Press said, "a telegram? I want a letter. Write me a letter! Let's have some . . ." He held his hands out, palms up.

"Efflorescence?"

"You got it."

I took the letter from him and, sitting there, wrote: "We at Belles Lettres want to know how we're doing. We put out a magazine every week, and sometimes we feel we're too close to get the big picture. But you're on the sidelines. You're a critic. Criticism is your business. We want you to criticize us. We want to know what you think about us. As you may know, we have a new editor. He is concerned about the impact his editorship has had on the magazine. So we would particularly like to know how our most recent issues strike you. We've taken the liberty of enclosing them for your perusal. We hope you can take a few moments from your busy schedule to help us. We think you will, because you may be helping American literature."

I handed it to Press.

"Now we're talking. This is a *letter*. Here!" He returned the paper. "Add this! Write it down! 'Enclosed find a check for $500. Keep it! Cash it! Whether you answer us or not it's yours. And thanks a million! I wish the check were for a million.' You got it?"

"I got it," I said.

"Give it to Selma!" he said, got up, and rubbed his breasts.

One critic, now in his seventies, who had made his name as a young man with a lyrical appreciation of late nineteenth-century and early twentieth-century American prose, called to ask what was up. I repeated what Press had said to me. "Yeah, yeah," he said, "but what does he want?" I said I honestly didn't know anything besides what was in the letter.

"Come *on,*" he said, "how can I answer you people if I don't know what's going on?" This irritated me, probably because he was feeling as helpless as I had. I said, "Why don't you just do what the letter asks and not worry about the subtext." He said we were a tricky bunch and he would figure the thing out for himself.

His lengthy reply, which was delivered by messenger the next day, ended: ". . . However it has been achieved, the general tenor of the writing has certainly become lighter and clearer. Whether this is due to a change of contributors, defter copyediting, editorial guidance before composition, or perhaps an awareness on the part of the contributors that a higher standard of prose will now and henceforth be required of them, it is hard to say. Perhaps a combination of all these reasons. But whatever the background, there is no doubt in my mind that Belles Lettres has been initiated into a new phase of its long, honorable, and immensely useful life."

Another critic phoned, also to find out what was up, except he went about it differently. He said he thought it was a brilliantly innovative move to bring "the more important contributors" into the editorial process. Whoever was responsible has shown a great sense of responsibility to the duties of his calling. I said the idea was Press's, which brought forth raptures from the critic. His letter, when it arrived, went: ". . . I have always seen Belles Lettres, as indeed I see every individual publication, in terms of its context, that is, as an organ of the cultural body. Any change in the body as a whole affects each part, just as any change in a part affects the whole. In respect to Belles Lettres in especial, it has been clear to me that it has been reaching into both the past and the future for its nourishment and its direction. As to my perception of the *new* Belles Lettres, I would say this: Belles Lettres, up and until the recent change of editorship, has fashioned its identity after the models offered by tradition; it valued and put to high purpose the lessons of convention and common understanding (literary, societal, political, etc.). And this has been good. Only through maintaining our connection with what we have been can we understand what we are. However, in the issues of Belles Lettres that have been sent to me I discern a definite shift of the center of gravity, so to speak, from the past to the future. What was a protector is becoming a prophet. We need both, of course; but perhaps at this juncture we need the latter more. My heart and hand go out to you in this exciting venture."

A third critic called to say that he was interested in responding to my letter, but if he was "to help the magazine through this difficult period of transition" he would have to be guaranteed certain reviewing assignments. He named six of the dozen most prominent titles of the coming season. Three were by writers I knew to be his friends and one was by a dedicated enemy. I said the most I could do was bring his name up when reviewers were being discussed. He said he was disappointed that I could not offer him a more attractive incentive. Nonetheless he would do what he could to help us out. In his letter he too found the new Belles Lettres full of merit.

All told, seven of the ten sent in critiques. Six were fulsome; one was a postcard: "Seems like the same old thing to me. Best wishes for change. Thanks for the check."

Nine of the ten critics cashed their checks. (Months later I ran into the one who hadn't. He said he recalled throwing away an unopened letter from Belles Lettres thinking it was a subscription solicitation. He wanted to know if he could get another check. I said he could try.)

When I turned the responses over to Press he was pleased. "Ho-*kay*! Pull out fifteen hundred words. We'll run it in the next issue."

"You're joking."

"I'm not joking. If we're doing good work and the critics want us to know about it there's no reason why everybody shouldn't know about it."

"Are you going to ask permission to publish these letters?"

"What's with permission? These are paid appraisals, like I took a ring to the jeweler."

"I don't think it's like that at all. The people had no idea you would publish what they said."

"Don't you think they said what they thought?"

"Frankly, no."

"See, that's the difference. You're suspicious, I'm not."

I could have called the critics and given them a chance to object. Instead I decided they deserved whatever they got.

Excerpts from the six letters filled page three of the next issue without a prefatory note, as if they represented a spontaneous outpouring of love. I heard only from the first critic. He now knew what was up, he said, repeating that we were a tricky bunch. "And *you,*" he said, "I'll remember *you.*"

The letters did not go unnoticed. New York magazine gave Belles Lettres the William F. Buckley Self-esteem Award. The New Yorker ran a cartoon by William Hamilton showing a man holding a copy of Belles Lettres and saying to his wife, "If you don't blow your own horn, no one else will blow it for you." The Village Voice, which found out how the letters came to be written, published an earnest exposé under the headline "Belles Lettres Pays for It."

Despite the publicity, Cyrus Tooling Jr. sent Press and the staff a recognition-richly-deserved memo. Ed Princeps called a meeting of the de-Press-ion committee, which concluded that Press was riding high and the committee should regroup and rethink. The only good that seemed to come from Press's triumph was that he stopped pushing me to get rid of the dead wood.

Then Press started being absent from the office, more than half of most days and some days the whole day. Lou Bodoni learned from Selma that he was spending the time in Mrs. Tooling's office. An ominous turn, we thought. Was a massacre in the works?

Thursday mornings the staff met in the editor's office to plan the upcoming issue. We usually had on hand enough copy to fill three issues. This gave us room to move around in. For instance, if a novel was scheduled for the first page, we would want nonfiction on the second, probably an essay on the third, and so on. The arrangement was grandly called architecture. Mr. Margin had been a meticulous architect. He not only worried about the effect of, say, following poetry with politics and politics with science ("We can modulate from the politics to the science, but not from the poetry to the politics. Perhaps if we go poetry-*science*-politics . . ."), he would also take into consideration the composition of the preceding issue ("Frank, didn't we have fiction on page five last week?" to which I might say, "But that was by a woman, this is by a man," to which he would say, "Yes, I see it, a nice variation." Then if he said to me on a subsequent occasion, "Frank, we had short stories on page five last week, also by a woman," I might say, "That's just the point I think we should make," to which he would say, "Yes, it's a comment, isn't it?"). Actually, I doubt if there were two readers in a thousand who consciously or unconsciously remembered Belles Lettres's architecture from one week to the next. But, as I say, Mr. Margin was meticulous.

Not so Press, who had only a journalistic concern with books, that is, with their subject matter and the renown of their authors. Being barely familiar with literary names and issues, he fastened on anything he recognized. Thus he would schedule on page one a second-rate novel because it was reviewed by a famous author, even though the author's brain and style had softened in recent years. When the choice was questioned Press would say, "The review's by . . ." and pronounce the name as if it were an argument. Beyond that, he composed the magazine by landfill. The strange thing was that, for all his negligence and Mr. Margin's care, Belles Lettres looked about the same.

As I say, that's what we did on Thursday mornings. It came as a shock when Press announced on this Thursday that we would be holding the first three pages open. When asked what the story was, he said he was not free to say, and when asked why, he said "security reasons." This mystery added to the fears of the staff, and that afternoon a de-Press-ion meeting was held in a corporate conference room. Ed Princeps reported to me later that the tone had been despondent and cautious—cautious because people were hoping to be among the survivors, if there were any.

Press took me to lunch the next day. He seemed tickled about something. He knew of the staff's meeting and claimed to be amused by their fears. As we talked I watched for the look of sadistic fun that a firing would have brought forth; all I saw was goosiness.

"Frankie boy," he said, "what do you know about Shakespeare?"

"Just what we all know."

"Have you read the sonnets?"

"Sure."

"All of them?"

"Yes."

"No you haven't."

"I haven't?"

"What would you say if I told you Tool and I have discovered nine lost Shakespeare sonnets?"

"I'd be speechless."

"What do you know about Shakespeare's sex?"

"Are we talking gender, genitals, or activity?"

"What he did."

"One sonnet specifically says that his male friend was 'pricked out for woman's pleasure' and not for him."

"Forget it! It's a whole new ball game," Press said. He had to wipe the corners of his mouth in his excitement.

XII

False Lies

COPIES OF WHAT CAME TO BE KNOWN AS "THE SHAKE-speare number" were sent, as usual, by the printer to the office two days before the issue was to hit the newsstands; and, as usual, one copy was flopped onto each desk by the messenger.

No heirs ever read a will with more attention than the staff gave that story. Ellie Bellyband's phone rang; without looking up she lifted the receiver an inch and let it fall. Others told callers to call back. And, while everyone read, Press strutted around saying, "Huh, huh? How about that?"

The introduction in outsize italic type filled page one:

WAS SHAKESPEARE GAY? Nine Newly Discovered Sonnets By the Bard Says He was

On April 2 the editor of Belles Lettres received an unsigned special-delivery letter. It began by pointing out some facts in the peculiar history of Shakespeare's sonnets: that they were first published in 1609 in London, apparently without the cooperation of the author; that there was no known contemporary response to the publication, even though at the time Shakespeare's fame during his life was at its height; that the absence of response had led to the theory that the volume was suppressed; that the sonnets were largely ignored for a century, and in 1711 a London publisher reprinted them from the original volume. Since then they have not been out of print and in fact have stimulated much speculation and controversy; one of the most intensely debated questions was whether Shakespeare had a homosexual love affair with "the young man of the sonnets," generally conceded to be the third Earl of Southampton.

The letter pointed out that there are 13 known copies of the 1609 volume, none in private hands, and went on to state that a 14th had recently been discovered in a cache of Southampton's papers. The letter continued with the sensational claim that this 14th copy contained two loose leaves printed on both sides with nine unnumbered sonnets; the typeface and the paper, the letter said, were the same as those of the volume itself. Most of these sonnets describe or refer to explicit sexual acts between the author and the addressee.

The sonnets were being offered to Belles Lettres, which could subject them to whatever tests were necessary to establish their authenticity. The letter ended with the statement that the owner, who for the moment wished to remain anonymous, expected no remuneration. That would come, generously, if and when the volume was disposed of. In the meantime the owner was interested in sharing his find with the public through responsible publication.

It all sounded initially like a cross between a joke and a kidnapping.

However, on April 4 Belles Lettres received a call from a man who said he was acting for the owner. He would deliver in person photocopies of the sonnets. They were handed over the next day at lunch, with one proviso: that we do everything in our power to keep the matter secret until actual publication. The interest of the owner, the deliverer said, was in journalistic impact. We agreed with the condition, and we agreed with the purpose.

The poems were subjected to rigorous tests. The letter images were checked against one of the original volumes and were found to match, without exception. (See examples.) Obviously the two leaves had been printed from the same font. The premier Shakespeare scholar, S. Sewnbound, was engaged to examine the sonnets for internal evidence of authorship. His report appears below; he concludes that the sonnets not only might have been written by Shakespeare, they "could not possibly have been written by anyone else." Our second expert, Gary Cartouche, the respected statistician of Elizabethiana, examined the poems for word parallels with Shakespeare's other work; his findings, which also appear below, offer startling scientific confirmation of Mr. Sewnbound's conclusions.

The nine sonnets are shown here in two modes: a photographic reproduction of the pages, followed by a transcription of the sonnets into modern type, with spelling and punctuation updated for reader convenience.

Even those familiar with the 154 sonnets now in the canon may have trouble discerning the meaning of some lines. But, as Mr. Sewnbound points out, this perhaps more than any other factor establishes their authorship. "Who but William Shakespeare," Mr. Sewnbound says, "would have the audacity to compose the sonnet beginning 'Bestir thyself . . .'?" Many lines in these poems were written in the private language of lovers and refer to experiences shared only by them. On the other hand, many lines and some whole sonnets are only too clear in their import.

The questions arise, Why were these sonnets not bound into the original edition and how did they get into this newly discovered copy? The surmise of the owner, as reported to us, is that the publication of the 154 sonnets, being unauthorized by Shakespeare and possibly embarrassing to him and to Southampton, may have gotten the printer into serious trouble with the Stationers' Company, the government-licensed guild of publishers; including the nine sonnets certainly would have. But a few proofs were struck for "special subscribers." Needless to say, this is as yet a theory only; it will no doubt be carefully examined by scholars.

In the meantime, Belles Lettres is proud to bring this momentous find to its readers and indeed to the world.

The illustration for this introduction was two magnified *T*'s, one captioned, "The initial letter from the first printing of Shakespeare's sixth sonnet, 'Then let not winter's ragged hand deface' "; the other, "The initial letter from Shakespeare's newly discovered sonnet, 'Thou asketh if I miss a woman's part.' " And, allowing for different inking, they did look alike.

On page two were the nine sonnets shown twice, as the introduction described: once in old type, *s*'s looking like *f*s, *v*'s like *u*'s, and *u*'s like *v*'s, with odd capitals turning up in the middle of lines; followed by the edited version:

Tomorrow bring thy bed for my bed's sake
And let them empty lie in wed together.
They too that serve us should we lovers make,
Their pillows pressed with feather seeking feather.
Thy bed and thee have borne me silently,
Brave stoics both beneath the weighty charge
Except a creaking cry from it and thee
Whene'er the burden came especial large.
My bed and thine will talk of us in kind,

False Lies

Comparing privately our pointed part
That us with partless likenesses doth bind
And lifteth like a crane a loving heart.
If these two friends refuse to parted be
What place couldst thou lie down except by me.

This love that nature did deny the means
Or given means too much for it to prove
Has spite largesse enacted moving scenes
And wholly claimed the name and deed of love.
Thou foundest overreaching for my heart
Instead the fevered boneless new-made limb
That did with pearls of pleasure early part,
Unclosed, exhausted, spending at the rim.
Beheaded, senseless, shrunken to a wen,
My shamèd, shameless will with virtue filled
And longingly took up the task again
To sit upon the stool before it spilled.
Although we vainly issue would create
We spawn our pleasure thus whene'er we mate.

Last night when thou took hasty leave of me
And nox's winking candles showed thee home
I sent a dream to follow fast on thee.
It met instead beneath the solless dome
What thou had sent abroad, a dream of thine,
To search in earnest for newfangled love.
Seeing my dream but knowing not 'twas mine,
Thy faithless dream did lastly faithful prove.
Why dost thou send thy lusty dreams of prey

Through open casements like a rajah dighted?
Do not my kisses thine in full repay?
Hath not my love thy love in full requited?
Thou claimest not to give thy dreams command.
Remain with me and they'll be kept in hand.

Rebel, refuse, recoil, renounce, reject.
This is the season of our soft retreat.
No hell do cowards but themselves reflect.
Will we with others e'er our love repeat?
Is this how love's good fortune is repaid,
With rank regret, revolt, revenge, remorse?
O be it not to jealous ears relayed
That we to harsh reproach have no recourse.
No pardon we reclaim nor just reprieve.
We love have slain and must our souls resign
To punishment and punishment receive.
Thus do we love's revenge ourselves refine.
But could we raise the shy retired lover
We might our former innocence recover.

Not only does thy voice delight mine ear,
So does thy step approaching near to me.
Not only is thy form to mine eye dear,
Thy very shadow is an ecstacy.
Not only do thy lips content my lips,
Thy rainbow is forlain against my heart.
Who breathes thy breath the scent of summer reaps.
As sweet thy hair, thy skin and every part.
And last the dumb and faceless gift of touch,

That one that plants and bully billiards know.
No other sense is pleasured half so much
By all the rounds and hollows thou dost show.
Each of my senses thou dost gratify.
What can I do to thee but cling and sigh?

Bestir thyself to see day's constancy
While moons recline beyond the midnight gate,
A token sent for further love of thee,
Intending to forgo a morning fate.
False lies to flame the fire thus between
Entirely given and withheld from sight,
Dissentious tears the futile state and mean,
Why what is done can grant our evil quite.
O tear the unkind morsel from his hand
And bind the wounds of puissant destiny,
For whether five or sixty or a stand
Is not for mortal sale or second fee.
Then take what cold return these lines can give
And I shall prosper, men the while will live.

Have I been brother to thee? I and less.
And sister when I lip thee on the cheek.
And uncle have I been in nepotness,
And often wife obedient and meek,
A father most when needed thou consent
To aye thy heart's request despite thy head,
A cousin in thy moods of merriment,
A daughter with devotion filièd.
Take all these roles I gladly offer thee

And, walled with wit, manure thy delight.
There is one other love I do supply
That fondest is when hidden most from sight,
The love that fills the rosy cup of flesh,
May it forever flow with liquors fresh.

There is a part of me that I would hide
Within the tender haven of thy flesh
And let it there for countless ages bide
To find it awed and call men in the mesh.
No sooner am I settled in this haven
Than heaven thou dost cruelly take away
Explaining that salvation although given
Is given after death has taken sway.
If ardent lovers sin when they do love
Our paradise anon will be a hell.
Should we not paradise today approve,
Our pains tomorrow easier to quell?
If this conceit convinces thee tonight
Remain I pray thee ever in my sight.

Thou asketh if I miss a woman's part
That, soft and cleft, doth open and invite?
My consolation now is in thy heart,
An organ giving all a woman's might.
In further recompense thou hast besides
A rowdy, rising, rousing thing that fills
And swells and wets and ebbs like ocean tides,
And this my lady yearning ever stills.
The while do I of dugless bosom tire?

I have thy mouth to satisfy my lips.
I have thy eyes to nourish my desire.
I have thy bottom for my fingertips.
I do not count thy beauties in a score.
All joyous things thou art to me and more.

Some of the fast readers when done began again. Others flipped back and forth, frowning. "Horseshit!" Barry Vellum shouted. "Fabulous!" Virginia Wrappers shouted. "Shut up!" someone else shouted, and the reading went on. After ten minutes people began talking. Three or four gathered around my desk. My phone rang. It was Mr. Margin. He had gotten his copy at his apartment by messenger.

"Have you seen it?" he said.

"Yes. What do you think?"

"I don't know, Frank. The pictures of the type look convincing. But there's something wrong."

"You mean it doesn't sound like Shakespeare."

"No, some of it does. But it also sounds like the efforts of a few clever people at a party. 'Rebel, refuse, recoil, renounce, reject.' Would Shakespeare have written that?"

"He wrote, 'Never, never, never, never, never!' Are you home? Can I come over?"

I read the whole thing again in the cab, including the two expert defenses.

S. Sewnbound, as the introduction said, had no doubt about the authorship: "Who but a supremely confident artist would have attempted the wordplay of 'Rebel, refuse, recoil, renounce, reject'? In Shakespeare's famous Sonnet 135 the word 'will' (the initial letter capitalized and not) appears 13 times to the reader's amazement and admiration. In 'Rebel, refuse . . .' there are no less than 24 iambic words beginning with 're'! And who but the Bard in his sonnet of the five senses, 'Not only does thy voice delight mine ear,' would have referred to touch as the sense that 'plants and bully billiards know'—plants with their connotation of pubes, billiards with their immediate suggestion of testes? But the masterstroke: '*bully* billiards'—bully with its original meaning of 'lover,' and its later, now also obsolete, meaning of 'pimp.' And over both, a hearty maleness and the sense of bodies colliding."

"The reason," he went on in another passage, "that Shakespeare's sonnets have interested commentators to such an extent is that one senses a mystery. For all their openness of feeling, something was missing. What was missing, it is now clear, is contained in these newly discovered poems. We have at last the reason for the poet's manifest tenderness, exaltation, and anguish.

"The imagery of male love is overwhelming throughout. One is tempted to say stifling. Yet in its very excess it is Shakespearean. Also Elizabethan. If Shakespeare had never existed and we had discovered these unsigned poems we could without a quaver of doubt place them in the late 16th or early 17th century, excess being of the essence of things Elizabethan."

Excess, I thought, was also of the essence of things Sewnboundian.

The poem beginning "Bestir thyself . . ." was "by far the most striking of the nine, perhaps the most striking of all of

Shakespeare's sonnets, with its glittering symbols, rocking balances, stunning oppositions, and surreal intermix of the abstract and concrete. 'False lies' becomes one of the most thought-provoking phrases in the Shakespeare canon. What *is* a false lie? Is it the deceptive intention that proves doubly revealing? Is it the lie that lies twice because it betrays love. Is it, when its paradox has been solved, the simple truth, like the intricate equation reduced to A equals A? Or is it all these? Knowing Shakespeare, I would say surely all these."

Gary Cartouche's computer-aided article was not so interesting but just as curious. He pointed out that Shakespeare's work, until the discovery of these poems, ran to 884,647 words; his vocabulary to 29,066 words. Thus arithmetically each word appears 30.435801 times. This, of course, is far from the actual case. The word *the* appears 27,457 times, while other words appear only once. "Shakespeare's genuine works contain," Cartouche says, "an unusually high proportion of these 'unique' words. Consequently any work with a credible claim to Shakespeare's authorship must contain a reasonable number. The nine sonnets satisfy this important criterion admirably," and he listed the words that did not appear elsewhere in Shakespeare.

His strongest evidence, however, concerned the rhymes. "A rhyme in a poem is like a chord in music. What do we listen to first in identifying a composer but his chords? The new sonnets consist of 126 lines, therefore 63 sets of rhymes. One of these (part/heart) appears three times, another (prove/love) two times; therefore there are 60 different rhymes in the nine sonnets. In the 154 sonnets these appear 68 times, an incredible coincidence to be accounted for in any way other than by Shakespeare's authorship."

There was something wrong with the logic of that, but I couldn't figure out what it was.

Mr. Margin was quite excited when I arrived. His robe was untied, and he was barefoot. He started right in: "This one that Sewnbound likes so much, 'Bestir thyself to see day's constancy,' it doesn't mean anything, it doesn't even parse."

"I thought that one sounded pretty good."

"Frank! Poetry is more than sound. Right now I'm looking up words in the dictionary. If I can find just one that definitely came into existence after Shakespeare's time we'll know it's a fake. There's *nepotness,* which didn't exist then or since, but Shakespeare does make words up."

"And *'filièd.'*"

"I thought that was rather clever," Mr. Margin said.

"Did you ever hear of *forlain?*"

"I have it right here." A volume of the Oxford English Dictionary lay open on a coffee table. Mr. Margin read from it: "'Of a woman: That has lost her chastity. Also, as a term of abuse for either sex.' There's a citation from the year 1290, 'A woman that was sunful . . . and for-lein.'"

"If *forlain* means that, what does 'Thy rainbow is forlain against my heart' mean?"

Mr. Margin pronounced it variously like an actor: "'Thy *rainbow* is forlain against my heart.' 'Thy rainbow is *forlain* against my heart.'" Then he said, *"Rimbaud and Verlaine!"*

"What?"

"Rimbaud and Verlaine. Rain*bow* and for*lain.* Wait!

Wait!" He snatched up his copy of Belles Lettres and after a moment read, "'No hell do cowards but themselves reflect.' Noël Coward!" He went back to Belles Lettres and in no time shouted, "'And, walled with wit, manure thy delight.'"

"Walt Whitman!" I shouted. "Press is dead."

"Long live the press!"

"Press is dead. Long live the press!" we chanted in unison and soon were dancing around Mr. Margin's living room. His Colombian maid looked in, and we danced with her too.

It took us half an hour to find the hidden homosexuals in eight of the nine sonnets. The ninth—I forget now which one it was—resisted us; it wasn't until the puns became a public guessing game that we got it.

We talked strategy for an hour. Then I phoned Selma to see how things were going at the office. At that very moment Press was being interviewed for the seven o'clock news. I wanted to be sure the story could not be withdrawn before we went to see Cyrus Tooling.

XIII

The Gay Deceivers

Cyrus Tooling's secretary said he had someone with him. We told her to tell Mr. Tooling that it was urgent. She asked if she might inquire into the nature of our business.

"Say 'Shakespeare,'" I said.

"That's all?"

"Just do it!" Mr. Margin said, and she did it.

Mrs. Tooling and Press were in the office with Tooling. I was amused at how passive and respectful these two bullies had become. They all held copies of Belles Lettres. So did Mr. Margin and I, except ours were annotated.

"So what do you think, you two?" Tooling said to us. "I think it's a big deal. But it's dirty. I don't like Belles Lettres to be dirty. We have magazines that are supposed to be dirty. Belles Lettres is a class act. I'm not saying they shouldn't have done it. I'm not even saying they should have shown me first, because, frankly, if they had, I would have said no. I would have said, you want to print this dirty stuff, print it in Fille. Better, in Garçon."

"Mr. Tooling," Press said, "we're talking Shakespeare. Right after the Bible comes Shakespeare."

"I know. I'm just saying I wish this big deal were in good taste."

"Cy," Mrs. Tooling said, "someone had to publish this filth, so why not us? . . . You agree with that?" she said to me.

"Not entirely," I said.

"You a prude?"

"Not really."

"A homophobe?"

"Not particularly."

"So why?"

"Maybe Mr. Margin should explain. He feels that Shakespeare didn't write these poems."

"What's the matter, Margin?" Press said, "You know more about Shakespeare than Sewnbound? So there'll be people who don't think it's Shakespeare, there'll also be people who do. There'll be all kinds of opinions, and maybe it will never be settled. So what? In the meantime these will be known as 'the Belles Lettres sonnets.' I call that *publicity*."

"Marge," Mr. Tooling said, "if I get you right, you don't think Shakespeare was . . ." He tipped his open hand back and forth. "For me it's also hard to believe. Shakespeare! Who's next? . . . So, all right, what's your angle?"

Silently Mr. Margin gave his copy of Belles Lettres, open to the sonnets, to Tooling. I gave mine to Mrs. Tooling and Press. We had underlined the eight puns and beside each written the man's name, dates or approximate dates, and the word *homosexual.* I could tell from their stony looks that Press and Mrs. Tooling got it right away. Mr. Tooling was not far behind.

"So?" he said to his wife and Press.

They said nothing.

"So?"

Still they said nothing.

"Do you want me to open the window and you can jump? Or maybe I should jump. Let me ask you a simple question. What did you do to check this?"

I was surprised at how gently he was speaking. Then he screamed, "Talk!"

When they didn't answer, he lowered his voice again: "How did you check it?"

"We had an expert examine the typeface," Press said, "and we got the two Shakespeare experts."

"That's in the magazine. Tell me, the man who brought you the papers, did you check him? Did you ask for references? What did he look like?"

"A small man," Press said.

"Okay, a small man. That's nice. Was he white, black, green?"

"White."

"So he was white. What color hair?"

"Black, and curly."

"A small white man with black, curly hair. What color eyes?"

"Blue," Press said.

"Now we're getting somewhere. A small white man with black, curly hair and blue eyes."

Mr. Margin spoke up: "Did he wear an open shirt and loafers?"

"I think so."

"Marge, you know who this is?" Tooling said.

"I think it was the copyboy who used to work here, actually a grown man named Folio. Did he talk like a racetrack tout?"

"Yes, he did," Press said.

"Oh, so let me get this straight," Tooling said, "you took these dirty poems from a strange man who talked like a racetrack tout. He says they're by Shakespeare. So you say they're by Shakespeare and you put them in my magazine. Is that right?"

"That's not exactly . . ."

"Not exactly," Tooling said, "but close. Okay, now that we know what happened, let's see if we know what to do about it. Do you have any ideas?"

"We can print a retraction in the next issue."

Tooling's voice rose: "What issue? What makes you think there'll be an issue?" His voice subsided: "Any ideas, darling?"

Mrs. Tooling shook her head.

"You?" he said to me.

"I believe Mr. Margin has an idea," I said.

"I'm not surprised," Tooling said, leaning back in his chair with exaggerated calm. "Please, Marge, your idea."

"The story will be on television tonight, on the front page of The Times tomorrow. . . ."

"Excuse me," Tooling said. "The front page of The Times. Is that right, Newbold? Did The Times call you?"

"Yes, sir."

"Now *that's* publicity! Go on, Marge!"

"First let me say that under no circumstances would I condone lying. Perhaps to avoid a positive evil, to foil a villainous act . . ."

"Please, Marge, the idea!"

"Well, tomorrow morning, when the follow-up stories are being written and more experts are being asked for their opinions, we announce that it was all a joke, and to prove it there are the hidden names in the poems. We were merely making a comment on the Hitler diaries, the Howard Hughes autobiography. In fact we're surprised that everyone didn't get the joke immediately. By the time the issue is on the newsstands the whole world will know we fooled some pretty smart people, or people who thought they were pretty smart. . . ."

I lifted my hand slightly from my knee. Mr. Margin noticed the movement and stopped talking.

The four of us sat in silence for perhaps a minute, until Mr. Tooling pointed at his wife and said, "Is this a good idea?"

She nodded.

He pointed at Press. "Is this a good idea?"

Press nodded.

"Marge, you handle it! Also do me a favor and take over the magazine until further notice. Okay?"

Mr. Margin nodded solemnly.

"And you help him!" he said to me.

"Yes, sir."

"Okay, go! . . . And you two," he said to his wife and Press, "stay!"

We heard the shouting at the elevator.

Mr. Margin and I went to the executive dining room for a celebratory drink and then back to his apartment. The first thing we did was phone Art Folio. I tried a little deception on him. I congratulated him on the scam.

"It wasn't mine, babes."

"That's not the way I heard it," I said.

"I was just the delivery boy. I mean, like always."

"The way I understand it, Art, if you hadn't done it exactly right it wouldn't have worked at all."

"You know what they were afraid of?"

I said, "What?" although what I wanted to say was, "Who? Who?"

"They were afraid I'd take money. They kept telling me if I took money we'd all go up for fraud. I'm no dummy. But they were afraid."

"You must all be happy as clams."

"I haven't seen either of them since we did it. So, babes, say hello to everybody. See you in the papers."

Mr. Margin thought the other hoaxers—we now knew there were two of them—were probably college students Folio had run into as a bookie. But I remembered that Chuckle Faircopy at a de-Press-ion meeting said that he was working on a secret scheme. I called him at Belles Lettres.

"It was you, wasn't it?"

"Of course," he said. "Who else could have done it?"

After I told him what had happened with Mr. Margin and me and asked him to say nothing to anyone until we had made our announcement, he revealed the details. Once he had the idea it took him a week to write the sonnets. "The first five took a night apiece. Then I realized I could get away with at least one that made no sense. That took ten minutes and sort of loosened me up for the rest. Sewnbound makes me think the ten-minute sonnet is pretty good."

"They're all good, Chuckle, perfect for their purpose," Mr. Margin said from the extension.

The mechanics worked this way. Ben Boards cut up, letter by letter, twenty or so sonnets from a facsimile edition of the 1609 volume, then "composed" the new poems the way an old-fashioned printer would, except that he used a tweezer and rubber cement instead of lead type. The results were photographically enlarged, retouched, and diminished to original size. It was the last product that was delivered to Press.

Mr. Margin's plan worked so well that the next day even members of the staff believed the hoax had been intentional. The publications that hadn't been stung by the story, like the news magazines, found it diverting. I heard that Newsweek was considering it for a cover and only cut back when they couldn't find out in time who had written the sonnets.

When the news got out, Chuckle and Ben became, you might justly say, famous. Mr. Tooling forgave them. Chuckle's novels were reprinted to good reviews and even made a few bucks. Ben was hired away by an ad agency that went in for fancy typography. Charles Hamilton, the memorabilia broker, sold the hoax materials to the University of Texas for $110,000, which Chuckle, Ben, and Art Folio divided equally. Mr. Margin's editorship was made permanent; he assigned his column to Virginia Wrappers, whose high-mindedness made it quite popular. Mrs. Tooling was retired to the Tooling estate in Purchase, N.Y. Press was shifted to Protean's industrial magazine Salle de Bain ("the smallest room in the house needs the most attention"), and at Mr. Margin's request the informer was sent over to help him. I quit to write this book, but before I left I managed to get Bobby Quarto, the copyboy who had pulled Press's tie, his job back for the remainder of his leave from Princeton. Claire Tippin didn't work out at Time, and Mr. Margin rehired her at $63,000 a year in some special capacity he tried to explain to me but couldn't make quite clear.

He and I see one another frequently, and I'm pleased to report he may very well have become a happy man.